"The Dummy Pass perfectly portrays the difficult reality of a child whose parents are the challenges school and life and necessary tool for any express the complexities of s child during this time. It prov can relate to, and empathis 8 years old or a parent going through divorce.*

Stone Priestly-Nangle
Sale Rugby Football Club

CW00736278

"An original, imaginative and sensitive book, The Dummy Pass beautifully captures the conflicting emotions of a boy desperately trying to find a firm footing as his world begins to fall apart.

Written from the heart, The Dummy Pass is aimed primarily at young readers and explores some of the consequences of marital breakdown as seen through the eyes of a keen, young rugby player. It is thought provoking yet reassuring, and will strike a chord with anyone, young or old, who finds themself in a similar situation."

Mary Ballingall,
Retired Teacher

The
Dummy Pass

Patrick Smith

Foreword
Paula Crowhurst

Publications

British Library Cataloguing-in-Publication Data.

A catalogue record for this book is available from The British Library.

ISBN: 978-1-913579-30-2 (Paperback)

ISBN: 978-1-913579-31-9 (ebook)

Publisher: Ladey Adey Publications, Copperhill, 1 Ermine Street, Ancaster, Lincolnshire, NG32 3PL, UK.

Cover Picture by Abbirose Adey of Ladey Adey Publications.

Goal Post Illustrations by Joshua Smith.

The Author has done everything to ensure accreditation of copyright of other's work. The Author accepts full responsibility for any errors or omissions.

This book is fictional and from the author's imagination. For dramatic and narrative purposes, the book contains fictionalised scenes, composite and representative characters and dialogue, and time compression. The views and opinions expressed in the book are those of the characters only and do not necessarily reflect or represent the views held by the author or publisher. No penguins were harmed in the production of this book.

Contact the author via www.patricksmith.uk

If you enjoyed this book, please add a review on Amazon for Patrick.

For Joshua. Always.

And L, M, J, E and P.

Foreword

For most families, divorce and separation come as a shock to children, with the physical and emotional upheaval it can cause. Many children then spend time walking on egg shells, feeling like they have done something wrong to cause their parents to split and that mummy and daddy don't love them any more.

It is hugely important that children are able to understand and express the feelings they are experiencing. What they believe to be true is as powerful and 'true' to them as the actual truth and internalised negative feelings can lead to physical complaints or behavioural problems.

In my work as a divorce coach I not only work with separating parents, but also help them and their children to communicate. For many children it can be easier to draw their feelings, rather than verbalise them. But to read about similar experiences for other children can also be very important. To realise this happens outside of them and their feelings are shared by others can be an important step to coping with and coming through this situation.

This can be especially true for boys. For men and boys, society creates an expectation of how they should behave and what masculinity is. They have been taught not to display emotion with phrases like, 'man-up', 'stop being a wuss' and 'boys don't cry!'. To have role-models that offer an alternative perspective is vital for the development of boys experiencing this situation.

As adults going through this process we must always try to think about what is best for the child(ren). While as a society, we must search for new and creative ways of supporting interpersonal relationships and strengthening the positive reinforcement of emotion, against stereotypes.

Books, such as this one, which demonstrate that the emotions felt are real, valid and painful are an important healing tool. It is also important to show, as this book does, that there can be light at the end of the tunnel and mature adult behaviour can help children successfully work through these difficult times.

Paula Crowhurst
Divorce Coach - (www.divorceseparationcoach.co.uk)
Author of *Keep on Swimming Freddie!* - a heartwarming story for young children to help them comprehend and handle the emotions they experience when their parents split up and divorce.

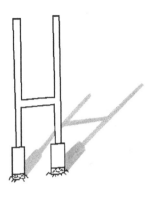

1

William's feet got tangled and he fell to the ground with a thud. He looked up, worried what the reaction would be, but there was nothing, no shouting. In fact, it was just silence. And the silence seemed to last an eternity.

Then William saw why. Instead of shouting at him, his dad was laughing. He was laughing so much that tears were streaming down his face and he couldn't actually make a sound. William was no longer scared. Actually, as he started to think what his fall must have looked like he too started to smile. Then he started to laugh. Pretty soon both William and his dad were laughing uncontrollably.

When they had both managed to stop laughing and regain their composure, William's dad explained the move to him again.

"What you're doing is pretending to pass the ball, but really you're trying to fool the opposition. Like this."

His dad's hands were a bit of a blur, going one way then the other, then the ball was hurled towards William. He didn't so much catch it as manage to cling on as it hit him in the stomach.

Despite nearly being winded, and occasionally falling over, William liked it when his dad played with him like this. It was rugby they were playing and his dad was teaching William a new move called the dummy pass. William had to act like he was just about to pass the ball to a teammate and then run off in the other direction. It was brilliant fun.

They were playing together in the back garden. His dad was so good at the dummy pass, it was as if he'd been doing it all his life. He started to make all the moves look even bigger and more exaggerated - he looked like he was dancing with the rugby ball. It looked a bit like the TV programme with the celebrities and the ball was William's dad's dance partner.

William started to laugh, so his dad did it even more. And then his dad threw the ball to him and immediately tickle tackled him - he tackled him to the ground, but tickled him at the same time. They both fell on the floor laughing.

"Ok," his dad said after they had tickled each other, laughed until they had tears in their eyes and then eventually both got their breath back. "Time for you to practise."

William took the ball and got up. He took a couple of steps forward with the ball out in front of him in both hands. Then he moved the ball across his body from right to left in front of his stomach, as if he was about to pass it to an imaginary teammate. At the last minute, he pulled it back into his stomach and turned to the right to run off.

It looked just about perfect, apart from the fact he fell over his own feet and landed on the floor with the ball spilling out of his hands. His dad laughed, again.

"Nearly," he said. "You were good, apart from the falling over bit."

William laughed. He knew his dad wasn't cross. As he laughed he remembered the joke he and and his friend Finlay had played on Tom earlier in the day. It wasn't the joke which had been funny, more Tom's reaction. He had shouted and yelled and then stormed off very dramatically. Both William and Finlay had almost fallen over they were laughing so much. Tom wasn't really angry and had come back a few minutes later. (He said he had done a lap of the playground and could hear them laughing even when he was in the far corner of the playground.) The three of them continued to joke about it for the rest of the lunch break.

William had only joined Northbrook School a few weeks ago, after he'd moved house with his mum and dad. They hadn't moved very far - it was about 15 minutes in the car from their old house - but it had meant William needed to change schools. He didn't mind. Although he'd had friends at his old school, and neighbours he sometimes used to play with, he didn't miss them. Now they had moved away, William realised they had just been friends of convenience. They were people he had played with because they were there, but they weren't proper friends, and the fact he didn't miss them now just proved that. On top of that, there were some people he really didn't miss - kids who used to bully him. So, overall, William was quite glad they'd moved.

The new school was bigger than his old school, and so it was a bit scarier. He still remembered being really nervous the night before his first day there. Looking back, it seemed strange to think about it - silly almost, as he had been fine. Most days he was more than fine, in fact today and the lunchtime fun was a good example of that.

William had been laughing about Tom's reaction all afternoon and on the way home too. Not even Stephen and Harry, the bullies at the new school (it seemed every school had them), could ruin his good mood. They hadn't been too bad today, but William was always a little bit nervous around them. Tom and Finlay told him to ignore them, but it wasn't always easy, especially after what had happened at his old school.

But today there hadn't been much from Stephen and Harry which needed ignoring. Harry had made some comments during the literacy lesson this morning which William felt were about him, but no-one else seemed to notice; and Stephen had pushed Tom while he was walking around the playground after the joke William and Finlay had played on him. But Tom hadn't fallen over and even he was chuckling so much he had been able to ignore it.

"Hello, sweetheart. Had fun?" William's mum asked him, interrupting his thoughts of school, as he came in carrying the rugby ball. She was going to kiss the top of his head, but then realised it was a mixture of sweat and mud, so she rubbed his arm affectionately. William liked it when she did that, he couldn't quite explain what it was, but she made him feel important to her.

But then she looked over at William's dad,

"What time do you call this?"

"What do you mean?" William's dad asked, taking off his muddy shoes.

"Well I thought you were cooking dinner tonight, Mark. You know I have to go out."

"We were just playing a bit of rugby together, love," Mark sighed. "Come on, Fiona, there's still plenty of time for dinner and for you to go out to that thingy of yours."

"You know how important this is to me, I don't want to be late," William's mum replied.

"Dad was just teaching me the dummy pass, weren't you, Dad?" said William, not wanting them to argue. "And I was good at it wasn't I, Dad?"

"You were great, when you weren't falling over," laughed his dad. "But what do you have to do to get even better?"

"Practise," said William. His dad always told him to keep practising. He said it all the time, for his spellings, his times tables, even about talking to people and making friends - and now about his rugby, too.

"Can I watch TV before tea?" William asked.

"Yes, but make sure you wash your hands and your face," said his mum. "In fact," as she looked at him again, "please change your clothes before you do anything - you're filthy."

William grinned and ran upstairs to the bathroom. As soon as he had gone his mum turned to his dad.

"I thought you said you were happy to cook tonight, and then I get home and you're messing about in the garden."

"It was just a bit of rugby. I'll cook now."

"But this is always the way with you, isn't it? You say you're happy for more responsibility around the house and then when I get home I have to remind you... again."

William didn't hear his dad's reply as he went into the bathroom, but he knew they'd keep going like this for ages. They were doing it more and more recently.

Of course they didn't know William knew about it, but he could tell, even if they weren't shouting. In fact, they never shouted and always smiled when he came into the room, or at least pretended to smile. But they were having more of these serious conversations about 'responsibility' or 'this relationship' and William hated it.

After he had washed and changed, he watched TV, a cartoon about a knight and his friend, a dragon. It was for little kids really, but William liked it.

When tea was ready they all sat down and ate together. It was yummy too - pasta with a kind of tomato sauce with lots of different bits in it like bacon and peppers and mushrooms - plus his favourite kind of pasta, the ones which looked like butterflies. When he was younger, he used to pretend they could fly into his mouth.

But the atmosphere wasn't yummy - they just sat in silence. William tried to start a conversation a couple of times, but he didn't get much response from either of his parents, just a nod, or a "hmm", so he stopped and ate silently.

As soon as it was over, they all got up and went in different directions. William's mum went upstairs to get changed.

"I'm going to be late!" she said, giving William's dad a funny look. His dad started to tidy the kitchen and William said he wanted to play a bit more rugby, so he went outside again.

After about fifteen minutes his dad called him inside, saying it was getting too dark to be in the garden any longer. Just as he washed the rugby dirt off his hands and face again his mum came downstairs.

"Right, I'm off then," she said. "You looked great playing rugby out there, well done. But make sure you be a good boy for daddy tonight and not too late to bed, it's school in the morning."

"You look pretty," William said and it was true, she did.

"Thank you, sweetie. Give me a kiss. Goodnight. And I mean it about not being late." She kissed him and put her jacket on. Just as she opened the door she shouted into the kitchen, "See you later." And William's dad mumbled something into the sink while he was washing up.

Once his mum had gone, and he had waved through the window as she drove away, William put the TV back on and watched some more cartoons.

"Ten minutes, sunshine, then it's time for you to go upstairs," said his dad. William groaned, but smiled at his dad too.

After his dad had read him a story and just before he was about to turn the light off William said,

"Dad, can I ask you a question?"

"Of course."

"When you were my age, were you any good at rugby?"

"No, not as good as you are. I played rugby when I was a bit older, but I played football when I was your age."

"How come you're so good at it now then?" William asked. His dad laughed.

"I'm much bigger and older than you, don't forget."

"I don't just mean the tackling - the dummy pass and all the other stuff that you can do."

"Well, I've had years to practise it."

"I don't think I'm any good at it," William said. "It's so hard and I keep falling over or dropping the ball."

"What's brought this on? I thought you were good tonight," his dad said.

"The boys at school are all *really good* and when we play in PE they're all much better than me."

"All of them?"

"No. But Stephen and Harry are. They say I'm rubbish. They say I'll never get on the school team."

"I didn't know your school had a team."

"Yeah, it's something to do with a local cup competition. And there are going to be trials soon. They're going to pick a team for the matches and to win the cup and everything."

"Well, you need to get to sleep so you've got enough energy for the trials. Don't forget the fact everyone has been playing rugby at your new school for a year already and you've only just started. I think you're *really good* too and you'd be on my team, that's for sure." His dad kissed him on the forehead.

9

"Sleep well and remember - I think you're a great rugby player." His dad kissed him again. "Love you, sleep tight."

"Love you too, Dad," said William as he snuggled down in his bed.

His dad switched the light off and in a few minutes William was fast asleep, dreaming about doing the dummy pass... except for some reason in his dream it was a normal pass but he was sucking on a baby's dummy while he played...

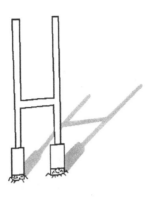

2

The next morning when William woke up, the sun was streaming through his bedroom window, and he could hear sounds from the rest of the house. A toilet flushed and he could hear water running from the taps, then a few minutes later the shower went on. Downstairs, in the kitchen, William could hear the kettle boiling and the radio was playing music. His parents were up and getting themselves ready for the day.

William knew it was time to get up, but he was in no rush. He wasn't in a hurry to get dressed and go to school. He didn't dislike school, but he certainly didn't like it much either. He dropped his head back onto the pillow, closed his eyes and continued to listen to the sounds of the house as he let the sunlight warm his face. Just as he found himself starting to drift off back to sleep, and dream about the dummy pass again, his mum came into his room.

"Wake up, sleepy head!" Time to get up and come down to breakfast." she said as she opened his curtains. William squinted and with a sigh got out of bed and went into the bathroom. Before long, he was downstairs eating.

Everyone was up and dressed and the three of them were at the table. It was a bowl of Cheerios for William, muesli for his mum and toast with marmite for his dad. The table was full and busy with all the plates, bowls, cereal boxes and jars of jam on it, not to mention the glasses and mugs

However, the people were silent.

William wasn't bothered about the lack of conversation - he was concentrating on making every spoonful he took from his bowl contain exactly five Cheerios, no more, no less.

"Right, I'm off." William's dad took the last bite of his toast, stood up, took his plate over to the sink then went upstairs to brush his teeth. A couple of minutes later he came downstairs again, kissed William on the top of the head, said goodbye and left for work.

William played with his Lego for a few minutes before he and his mum set off to walk to school.

William was in Year 5, so his mum had agreed she would walk with him for the first section of the route then when they met up with Tom and Finlay the three of them were allowed to walk the last section - through the park, past the playground and into the school gates - together.

"Are you all right? You're very quiet this morning," his mum said to William, as they were walking up to the main road.

"I'm fine," he replied.

"Ok, but you know if anything's bothering you, you can talk to me or daddy, don't you?" William nodded, but he didn't want to talk about the fact that he thought his parents were sad and he didn't know how to help them. Or that he was worried their sadness might never get better. He didn't even want to think about, let alone talk about what might happen if the sadness got worse.

"Right then, hold my hand as we cross. Not yet... wait. Ok, now." They walked quickly across the road.

For the rest of the walk William's mum talked about what she was going to be doing at work that day and something about whether she should ask for a promotion or not. But William wasn't listening properly, he wasn't even sure what his mum's job was.

After about fifteen minutes, they came to the churchyard and walked along the path which cut through the centre of it. Passing through the churchyard saved them over five minutes compared to the route along the road around the edge of the church grounds. William was pleased they didn't have to walk any further, but he was glad it was light in the morning and they weren't going through the churchyard in the dark. Ahead of them waiting on the corner, near the entrance to the park, was Tom.

"Tom!" William shouted and ran towards him.

Tom had been William's first friend at his new school. On the very first day of the new school year, which had been William's first day at Northbrook, William had sat next to Tom. They had been told to write their names on their new school books in silence, but Tom had talked, or rather whispered to William, all the way through it.

By the time first break came around William knew all about: Tom's hamster, which had died, about his favourite Lego model, the football team he supported and how his older sister had got into trouble in the holidays. William had managed about five words in that time, but they were already best friends.

Tom was waiting on his own, but as William and his mum reached him, Finlay appeared as well. He only lived round the corner, so he would wait and peer out of his kitchen window until he saw everyone arrive and only then would he come rushing out. On cold days he sometimes waited even longer. Finlay and Tom had been friends for as long as they could remember; their mums were friends too. As soon as William made friends with Tom, he was automatically friends with Finlay too.

William's mum waited to check the three of them were ok and with a final wave and a shout of,

"Have a good day at school!" she turned and started to walk back the way she had come.

"Thank you. You have a good day, too, Mrs Brown," Tom replied. William and Finlay rolled their eyes at Tom, but he spoke to William's mum like that almost every morning.

The three boys only had another five minutes or so to walk. Tom had watched a TV programme about monkeys last night, so he spent the whole five minutes excitedly telling the other two about it. According to Tom, the best bit was when the monkeys had a fight and one of the younger males had nearly killed an older male. Tom was suggesting that maybe the schoolboys could do that to a teacher, but William thought he was only joking - or at least he hoped he was only joking!

As they got to the entrance to the school, all three boys noticed a sign stuck to the railings:

NORTHBROOK SCHOOL RUGBY TEAM
YEARS 5 & 6
Trials on Friday After School

Mr Giles

"We should definitely try out for the team," Tom said enthusiastically. "It would be epic." With that, he ran into school pretending to pass an imaginary rugby ball to the other boys and pretending to tackle almost everyone else. Just as he reached the main entrance doors, he scored a 'try' and was celebrating along the corridor when the school bell rang, and it was time to go to their classrooms.

Finlay was in a different class to William and Tom, but the two of them didn't have time to chat in the first lesson. They had to do numeracy and had a series of questions to work through in what Miss Heath called 'Quiet Concentration'. This hadn't stopped Martha from suddenly squealing at one stage in the middle of the lesson, which had caused everyone else to giggle and managed to make the classroom neither quiet, nor full of concentration. When Miss Heath went to investigate it turned out that Sharon had pinched her under the table and the two of them had to be separated for the rest of the lesson.

It was break time when the boys finally got together again and could discuss what they had seen. Although they could remember what it had said, they had decided to go and look at the sign again, just to make sure.

They went down to the PE changing rooms, knowing it would be on the notice board there too. As they all stood there reading it again, Tom asked William,

"Are you going to go for it then?"

"Dunno."

"You should, you love rugby, and your dad can help you out a bit too."

"Yeah, but I've never played for an actual team or anything," William protested. "That's just me and my dad messing about in the back garden. And anyway," he continued, "this will be with Year 6 as well. What about all the bigger boys?"

"If you're scared of getting hurt, then maybe you shouldn't go to the trials," said a voice just next to William. It was Stephen. In their excitement, they hadn't seen Stephen and Harry standing next to them, looking at the poster themselves.

William didn't say anything. He just looked at Stephen who had a look of concern on his face, but not real concern, it was as if he was too concerned. The look Stephen had was the same as being told your pet hamster was about to be run over by a lorry. He couldn't keep it up and soon his face cracked and he started to laugh.

"It's alright, Harry won't hurt you too much, will you, Harry?" Harry grinned and pretended to rugby tackle William, which made William jump back in shock and made Stephen laugh even more.

As William stepped back away from Harry, he tripped over Tom's bag, which had been dropped in the middle of the corridor. He caught it with the heel of his left foot, knocking him further off balance, then as he continued to step backwards he tried to avoid standing on it with his right foot. That manoeuvre, combined with the stumble, meant that he took three more backwards steps across the corridor until he hit the wall opposite with his shoulder and slid down, ending up sitting on the floor.

Stephen was laughing hysterically now. Harry smirked and sniggered. Tom and Finlay didn't know what to do. Stephen and Harry were between them and William, and they were too scared to push past them to check on their friend. As for William, he was still trying to work out exactly what had happened and was sitting in an awkward position on the floor of the corridor while his mind was trying to catch up with his body.

Stephen controlled his laughter and stepped up to William, towering over him, with Harry - who was taller than Stephen anyway - standing directly behind him. They made a menacing sight for William who was looking up from the floor.

"Anyway, you're rubbish so you'll never get in the team. I wouldn't bother if I was you," he sneered. As they swaggered away, they kicked Tom's bag down the corridor and laughed again.

Tom and Finlay rushed over to William and helped him up. He wasn't really hurt, although his shoulder was throbbing a little where it had hit the wall, but he was a bit shaken up.

William felt that if he couldn't even cope with those two bullies, how would he be able to cope with a rugby match? He started to convince himself that the best course of action would be to ignore the trials altogether.

Tom and Finlay could see the worried expression on his face and tried to cheer him up.

"What a pair of idiots," Tom said quite loudly, although not loudly enough to be heard by Stephen and Harry as they continued down the corridor.

"Are you ok?" asked Finlay.

"Yeah, yeah, I'm fine. Sorry about your bag, Tom."

"Don't worry about that," Tom said. He put his arm around William's shoulder to comfort his friend, "and don't worry about those idiots. You'll get in the team no problem," he said.

"He's right," said Finlay. "You shouldn't let them put you off. You should at least go to the trials."

William still wasn't sure, but Tom was. "That's settled then," said Tom.

"I'll come with you and Finlay can watch us run rings around all the bigger boys." William rubbed his shoulder and kept quiet.

Tom was small and energetic, with a blond mop of unruly hair and an infectious smile. He was always up for a challenge or an adventure. He was a quick runner too, but William thought he was almost certainly too small to be a rugby player.

Finlay was taller and quieter. He suffered from asthma and so wasn't very interested in sport, especially cold winter sports out on the playing fields. He was a great swimmer, but everyone knew he wouldn't want to play rugby; the other two didn't even need to ask.

Physically, William was somewhere between the two. He was taller than Tom and although probably not as quick, he was stronger. He really enjoyed spending time with both Tom and Finlay. He loved racing across the school playground with Tom as he set off on another imaginary adventure, and he loved sitting and talking to Finlay about TV or playing Top Trumps with him.

However, William was always slightly amazed the three of them could stay friends because they were all so different, especially Tom and Finlay. Yet, they had been friends forever, they had even played together as babies. There was something protective in the way they were with one another, William knew that the two of them would be friends for life. He hoped they would be friends with him for life, too.

The rest of the school day was quite boring. Geography was the next lesson after break, and they had learned about how mountains are formed. At lunch time, after eating their sandwiches, the three of them carefully avoided Stephen and Harry by sitting in the library. The only downside to that was they had to be quiet (which was very hard for Tom) so they had played with Finlay's Top Trumps. They hadn't talked about rugby at all over lunch and William and Tom didn't get chance to talk about it during the afternoon lessons either. In fact, William thought Tom had forgotten all about it, until the end of the school day.

"William's going to go to the school rugby trials on Friday, Mrs Brown," shouted Tom to William's mum as she met the boys after school. "Don't let him forget his kit." It turned out Tom hadn't forgotten about it after all. William didn't argue when his mum asked him if he wanted to try out. So, Tom had decided it for him; William was going to the rugby trials.

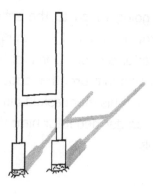

3

Friday had been a long day and William was settling down to his favourite evening of the week. Tea was always a Chinese takeaway which his dad picked up on the way home from work, and for some reason both his mum and dad seemed to be happier on Fridays.

His dad always complained about being tired from work, but on Fridays his mum didn't tell him off for it. Maybe walking through the door with a Chinese takeaway was the magic solution. William didn't mind, as long as he got his fried rice and chicken with cashew nuts. He'd tried some of the dishes his mum and dad had, but he didn't like them, they were too spicy, so he stuck to the chicken with cashew nuts... and of course, the prawn crackers.

"Get your hands off those!" William always snuck a couple of prawn crackers as his mum was serving the food up.

"Right, if you take another one you won't get any with your tea," said his mum, but William knew she was only joking. This was another part of the Friday ritual.

"Come on, Mark! It's ready," William's mum shouted upstairs to his dad.

"Coming," came the reply and then a few seconds later they heard footsteps on the stairs and his dad came into the kitchen having changed out of his work suit and into jeans and a jumper. "Right then, let's eat."

The happiness lasted for nearly an hour, but once the food was finished and the conversation had dried up, things went back to normal. William's dad stood up with his wine glass and was about to leave the kitchen and head upstairs to the room he used as his office. William got up too, to watch some TV before bedtime.

"Oi, you. You can help me clear this table before you disappear," William's mum said to him. But as William picked up one of the heavy dishes he dropped it back onto the table and winced.

"Ow!"

His dad turned round and came back to the table,

"Careful, Champ."

"Sorry, Dad, I just forgot about my sore fingers."

"Why, what's happened to them?"

"They got stood on at the rugby trials."

"Oh heck, the rugby trials were today, I completely forgot, how did it go?"

Both William's mum and dad sat back down again and as his dad gently pressed William's fingers to see if they were broken. William winced some more and told them all about his day and what happened at the rugby trials.

Over lunch both Tom and Finlay had been pestering William.

"You are going, aren't you?" they had both asked repeatedly.

"I think so, but you're coming too aren't you, Tom?" William had asked.

"I can't. I've got to go straight home because we're going away for the weekend," Tom said.

"Did you even ask if you could go to rugby?"

"Nope! I only said I'd go with you to make sure you go," said Tom. "I don't really like rugby. And I think I'm too small anyway. But you'll be amazing at it."

William was annoyed. He wasn't sure he wanted to go anyway, and now Tom wouldn't be there, he was even less sure. Tom and Finlay didn't mention it again over lunch, but in Maths, the final lesson of the day, Tom whispered to William,

"Listen, I'm sorry but I wouldn't be any good anyway. But you will. I think you're going to be picked for the team. I reckon you could be the star player."

So as the bell went William picked up his sports kit and headed off to get changed instead of going straight to after school club, which he normally did on a Friday.

There were about 35 boys all getting ready and there was an atmosphere of nervous tension in the changing rooms. Stephen and Harry were both there, so William got changed at the other end of the room.

They all ran out onto the pitch and were soon split into four groups. Each group was practising a different skill - passing, tackling, kicking and scrums. Some of the Year 6 boys looked huge to William and he wondered how he'd ever tackle any of them.

"What position do you play?" It was Simon Evans, one of the boys in William's year. He wasn't sure they'd ever actually spoken to each other before, but now he was asking William a question. The thing was, William didn't know the answer because not only did he not know the names of any of the positions, he had never played in a rugby match before.

"Are you a forward or a back?" William just shrugged.

"Do you play in the scrum or not?" Simon was getting impatient now.

"Oh, not. I think."

Simon sighed and walked off, but as he left he just said,

"You'd better practise your passing then." He pointed to a group over to William's left who were throwing a rugby ball to each other.

After the skills session, they had played a kind of game. Mr Giles, the teacher who was running the rugby team, started by explaining the rules and how you scored points at rugby.

"For those of you who have never played a match before," he said, "there are three ways to score points in rugby: a try, a conversion and a penalty."

Mr Giles went on to explain. A try was when your team puts the ball on the ground behind the try line - worth five points. After you had scored a try, your team then got the chance to score another two points by kicking a conversion - kicking the ball between the two upright posts, but over the bar which joined them. The final way of scoring points - by penalty - was worth three points. It was a kick, just like a conversion, but awarded by the referee if the opposition did something against the rules.

Once he'd explained the rules, Mr Giles divided the players into two teams and started the match. However, as they were playing, he regularly swapped players around and made them play in different positions, or on different teams. At one stage, William caught a pass and had run past a few players towards the try line. He thought he was doing well, but it was only when he was just about to put the ball down to score a try he realised he had run in the wrong direction as he'd just swapped teams.

William wasn't the only person at the trials who hadn't played much rugby before, but most of them, especially the Year 6 boys, definitely had. Soon after he had run the wrong way, he had another chance to run with the ball. This time he was running in the right direction, but just as he thought he had run past a Year 6 boy he was hit hard by a fierce tackle. William was shocked and lay there for a minute, but the Year 6 boy jumped up, took the ball off William, and ran off in the opposite direction. Unfortunately, just as he set off, he trod on William's hand, causing him to wince in pain.

Other than that, William hadn't touched the ball very often. He'd tried a dummy pass once, but had been tackled straight away anyway. Then the trials ended and they all went back to the changing rooms.

"Now listen, lads," said Mr Giles. "That was great. Thank you all for coming along. As you know we need 15 players for a team and five subs. So, 20 of you will get picked for our first match next Friday. The rest of you, there'll be another practice the following Friday, so please come along again and maybe you'll get picked for the next match. I'll put the team up outside the changing rooms in a couple of minutes, check it as you leave."

William got changed slowly. 'At least I tried,' he thought. He wasn't sure he'd come to the next practice; he didn't see the point.

There was a lot of excitement as boys went up to the notice board just outside the changing rooms. William heard Stephen and Harry showing off about how they were in the team, so he just walked around the group to go to after-school club.

"See you next Friday then, Will," said Simon as William walked past him.

"Yeah, right... Hang on, what?" But Simon had gone off with Stephen and Harry.

William made his way back to the notice board and as the crowd cleared he had a look at the sheet of names Mr Giles had pinned up. 20 names were listed on the piece of paper and there at Number 19 was 'William Brown' written in Mr Giles' handwriting - he'd been picked. Wow! He couldn't believe it!

$O \quad O \quad O$

"That's fantastic, sweetheart. Well done!" said his mum and gave him a kiss on the forehead.

"Knew you could do it, kiddo," his dad said. "So, what position will you play?"

William and his dad continued to talk about rugby for over an hour and even searched online for footage of old matches and tries which William's dad remembered watching.

They watched a World Cup match from before William was born. His dad was very keen for him to watch this particular match as England had won, but it was a bit boring for William. They had also watched England play in another competition called the Six Nations. His dad had even tried to remember old tries he had seen when he was William's age. William was pretty sure YouTube hadn't been invented back then, but his dad found some of the matches he was searching for. Although his dad was talking about the match, or the try, or even a dummy pass the main thing William noticed from all the old video clips was the funny haircuts they had.

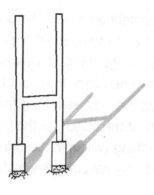

4

The next day they were going to the zoo as a family. William had dreamt about rugby all night and woke up grinning about the trials and being picked for the team. Then, when he remembered about the zoo, he grinned even more.

William loved penguins. He always had, ever since he was a little boy. He loved the way they walked, or waddled, how they slid around on the ice and how cute they looked. He always had to watch any TV programme with penguins in it and his mum still reminded him of the times he used to copy a penguin's walk when he was little. Now they were going to the zoo to see them in real life. He was so excited.

As soon as he opened his bedroom door, he stopped grinning. His parents were arguing. Even though he couldn't hear all the words they were saying, he could feel the argument.

"It's not my fault if I've got to work," he could hear his dad say.

"No! It never is, is it?" his mum shouted angrily in reply.

William ran back into his room and got back into bed. He could hear from his parent's voices that it was going to be one of *those* arguments, the ones which frightened him. He hid under the bed covers and tried to pretend it wasn't happening. They didn't happen very often, but these kinds of arguments were the worst. Both of William's parents were so angry with each other, they couldn't listen to or hear what the other one was saying, they were just screaming. Sometimes they even threw things and broke things. If they were really bad, then they would end with William's mum crying and his dad storming out of the house and driving off in the car. Once, in the old house, he was gone for nearly three days before he came back.

William used to cry under his bed covers when they were arguing like this, but he didn't want to cry today, he wanted to go to the zoo. So, he jumped out of bed and ran downstairs to get his breakfast. He tried to sing to himself as he went down the stairs, to distract himself from the shouting and screaming coming through his parent's bedroom door. But when he got into the kitchen, he realised he was shaking and it took him a couple of minutes to calm down enough to pour out the Cheerios.

Suddenly, all was quiet. William was eating and he couldn't decide if he should be more worried about the silence or the arguing. However, just as William was finishing his cereal his mum and dad came downstairs. They were smiling, but William could tell they weren't real smiles.

"Unfortunately, your dad can't come to the zoo today," his mum said, using the voice she used when she was trying too hard to be happy. "So why don't we ask Tom or Finlay if they want to come along with us?"

"Sorry, Champ," his dad said. "But I've got loads of work to do to get ready for a very important meeting next week."

"That's ok," said William bravely. He was disappointed his dad wasn't coming along and he was upset that his parents had been arguing again. But also, he was excited Tom and Finlay might be going with them to the zoo. They'd be able to laugh at the penguins together. Then he remembered Tom was away for the weekend, "I don't think Tom will be able to come, but Finlay might."

"Yeah, why not? We'll be able to natter while the boys look around." William's mum was on the phone to Finlay's mum. "No, I don't mind driving... of course... right then, we'll pick you both up in about 45 minutes." And with that she put the phone down.

"Finlay's mum thinks it's a great idea and she's gonna come too. I said we'd pick them up, so you need to go upstairs and get dressed right now."

William ran up the stairs and went straight into the bathroom to get ready. As soon as he was ready, he looked around in his room to find the little toy penguin his grandparents had given him for Christmas a few years ago. In the end, he found it under his bed and shoved it into his jeans' pocket. He ran downstairs, ready to go to the zoo.

"Look, I'm sorry," his dad was saying to his mum, "really I am." He too was washed and dressed and was holding a mug of tea to take upstairs to his office.

"Forget it, Mark. You can't make it right this time. We've had this planned for weeks." His mum turned and walked out of the kitchen, nearly bumping into William as he came down the stairs. She caught William and held him in her arms.

She took a deep breath, wiped her eyes, and said,

"Right then, trouble, let's get going." And they hurried out to the car.

Finlay and William sat in the back of the car chatting away through the journey to the zoo. Finlay had brought a pack of Top Trumps cards and they had tried to play with those for a few minutes, but the movement of the car made it hard for them to play, so they put them away and talked instead. They talked about their favourite superhero - which was the topic of the Top Trumps pack - their favourite TV programmes, how Tom never shut up and who was the nicest teacher at school.

William realised he had hardly ever talked to Finlay like this before. He supposed with Tom always around he and Finlay hardly ever had a chance to get a word in.

Their mums, sitting in the front seats, didn't talk as much. William's mum was busy concentrating on the driving and Finlay's mum was looking out of the car window.

Soon, they arrived at the zoo, or more accurately they arrived at the gates to the zoo. It took them another ten minutes to queue up to get to the car park and find somewhere to park. Those ten minutes were the worst bit of the journey with William too excited to talk to Finlay, he was just looking out of the car window and telling everyone to hurry up under his breath.

As soon as they parked the car William and Finlay jumped out and cheered.

"Yay!" "Penguins!" "The zoo!" "We're here!"

"Right, you two, calm down a bit," said William's mum. "There are a lot of people here, so we don't want you to get lost. You have to stay with us and not run off."

Finlay's mum nodded her agreement and gave a warning look at Finlay to try and calm him down, too.

"I know you want to see the penguins," William's mum continued, looking at him directly, "but let's do a quick tour of all the animals first. Then we can have some lunch and we can decide which animals we want to see again."

"Penguins!" shouted William and Finlay together. Finlay actually preferred the reptiles - the snakes and lizards - but William's enthusiasm made him excited to see the penguins as well.

"Okay, okay. After lunch we'll decide it's the penguins we want to see again." Both of the mums laughed at their over-excited sons.

The first animals they saw were the monkeys and of course both William and Finlay acted like monkeys around the pen. Or at least they did until one of the larger males ran towards them. The boys jumped out of their skin, but once they had calmed down all four of them laughed about it.

Next on the tour was the insect house. William was a bit bored, especially as it was so difficult to see most of the insects. They looked just like the branches they were sitting on. Finlay enjoyed it though and tried to get William interested in the stick insects.

After the insects, they went in to see the reptiles. Here, Finlay was in his element. He grabbed William's arm and took him around to all the different reptiles. He read all the information in front of each case, but it seemed to William he knew extra details for nearly all of them. Finlay was particularly interested in the lizards and he reeled off tons of facts about them.

"Did you know there are over five thousand different species of lizards?" It sounded like a question from Finlay, but before William could answer, he launched into more facts. "And some of them can regrow their tail if it falls off. They let it fall off if they are caught by a predator, so they can run away, then they just grow it back again. Wouldn't it be cool if we could do that to fool Harry and Stephen?"

William had enjoyed the reptiles far more than he expected to and it was because Finlay was able to tell him all those extra details. But, he was still impatient to get to the penguins. After all, this was the main reason for any trip to the zoo as far as he was concerned. However, before they got to the penguins there was another building which was full of different types of fish. Both boys groaned.

The mums tried to get the boys interested in the fish and read out all the details in front of their tanks, but after a couple of minutes they realised that it was a bit pointless.

"Come on then, let's go," William's mum said.

"Yay! Penguins!!!" Both boys yelled this and were shushed by their mums, although they chuckled at their enthusiasm.

The penguin enclosure was in the same building, but down a corridor and through two sets of double doors. As they went through the first set, they could feel the temperature drop and when they went through the second set, they all involuntarily shivered. The low temperature didn't particularly bother William or Finlay and they ran straight over to the enclosure.

The enclosure had lots of rocks and some caves towards the back, but it was dominated by a huge pool for the penguins to swim around in. The human visitors could look over the railing and see the penguins waddling around on the edge of the pool. They could also look through the knee-high glass portholes to see the penguins swim past under the water. To the right of where William and Finlay were standing was a flight of stairs which went down to a small viewing room which had one huge glass window showing the depths of the penguins' pool.

William and Finlay were already enjoying watching the penguins by the time their mums arrived to join them. The boys were popping up and down to watch the penguins waddle and swim. They would pick one penguin to watch and as it dived into the water and the two of them quickly dropped to the floor to watch the penguin swim. If they lost sight of it, or it jumped up out of the water again, then the boys would pop up and pick another penguin to watch.

"Can we go downstairs to watch?" asked William.

"Yeah, can we?" Finlay asked his mum.

Finlay's mum shrugged and so William's mum nodded. As they got to the top of the stairs she called after them,

"But down there or up here only. Don't go anywhere else."

The boys raced down the stairs; their excited chatter and laughter could be heard at the top of the stairs as well.

"I don't know why he's so excited about them, but it's great to see," said William's mum.

"At least they're a bit cuter than all the lizards that Finlay likes so much," said Finlay's mum. "They creep me out a bit, if I'm honest, but I don't want to tell him that. The penguins make me laugh, so I'm much happier here, despite the cold."

The boys watched the penguins dive down to the bottom of the pool and it seemed as if some of them were performing special tricks just for them as they twirled and somersaulted in the water.

As they sat, cross-legged on the floor, both of them staring into the water and watching the hypnotic display of the penguins, William said, "How come you know so much about all those lizards?"

"I've just read about them," Finlay replied. "I'm interested, so I read. Then that makes me more interested, so I read a bit more."

"I don't really know anything about the penguins, well, apart from the fact they live in the cold, they swim and they eat fish. I mean, I like them, but I don't *know* about them."

"If you read a bit more, maybe you could work out which type of penguin is your favourite and you could find out if they only eat fish or maybe some other sea creatures as well."

"Yeah, maybe," said William and he gazed up into the pool becoming mesmerised by the incredible movement of the penguin swimming closest to the glass.

After a few more minutes the mums came down the stairs. From half-way down Finlay's mum called out,

"Lunch!" Both boys jumped up, the spell of the penguins broken, and ran up the stairs to join them.

They bought some sandwiches from the kiosk and found a place to sit on the edge of the grass. The boys had a packet of crisps each and those were opened first, before the sandwiches. William and Finlay sat apart from their mums, a few metres away from them, and Finlay realised he hadn't asked about Friday's rugby trials.

"So, how was it?" he asked.

"It was ok." William admitted. "I didn't think I played very well at all, some of the other players were amazingly good. But weirdly, I've been picked as a sub for the first match."

"Hey, that's fantastic," said Finlay. "Well done! I knew you could do it. And considering you've not played in a match before, being sub is great. You can watch a bit first and work out more about the game."

"Yeah, suppose so," said William. He then told Finlay the story about running the wrong way, which made them both laugh.

"Can you eat some of your sandwich and not just crisps please, Finlay?" his mum called over to him.

"And the same for you," said William's mum.

"Thanks so much for inviting us," Finlay's mum said to William's mum. "It's ages since we've been here and to be honest, I'd almost forgotten how much Finlay enjoys it. Now his dad's not around, I sometimes forget to do stuff like this with him."

"How do you cope with just the two of you?" asked William's mum.

"It's okay most of the time. I'm definitely happier, but I'm also a lot more tired, which is why I usually forget the days out."

"Does Finlay see much of his dad? Sorry, I'm not sure I know his name."

"Andrew. And no, he doesn't. He's moved away with his girlfriend, and I heard a rumour that she's pregnant, so it'll probably make it even harder for him to see Finlay. To be fair, he's not a bad dad, just not around very often."

"It must be hard for Finlay."

"I think it is, although he seems to cope well enough. I try to encourage him to stay in touch with his dad, I think that's important, and of course he misses out on a few things, although he was never a rugby boy like William seems to be. But I think Finlay is happier now too, you know, now we're not arguing, although I'm not sure he actually realises it."

"You truly think he's happier?" asked William's mum.

"Definitely!" Finlay's mum replied. "And I know I am."

"Hmmm, interesting," said William's mum. She stood up and collected the used sandwich wrappers and crisp packets from everyone and walked over to the bin.

As she walked back, she looked at the boys in the middle of a game of Top Trumps and said,

"Are you happy playing here for a while or shall we go and see more penguins?"

"Penguins!" both boys yelled. They packed away the cards and the four of them went back into the penguin enclosure.

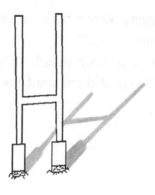

5

On Monday, Tom congratulated William for being picked in the rugby team as soon as he saw him. Finlay had already told Tom and as they walked over the field Tom excitedly explained how William was going to win the match for the school.

"Don't get too excited, I'm only a sub," said William.

"You'll start as the sub and then you'll come on and be the star player before the end of the match. Lots of professionals start their careers like that," said Finlay. Tom was more direct,

"Shut up! You'll smash 'em!"

Tom then told a story about how his older sister, Sophie, had started out as a substitute in her first match. William already knew she was a good rugby player, in fact she was the captain of the girls' team at the High School. Tom's story was about how his sister had scored two tries in her first match. As Tom got over-excited telling his story, William couldn't tell if Sophie became the team captain in the very next match, or if she scored another two tries, or both. But Tom was convinced that because his sister had done it, William was going to do it, too.

For the whole week Tom and Finlay were William's unofficial cheerleaders. They would tell him how great he was going to be when he felt nervous, and Tom never missed an opportunity to remind a teacher, or the rest of the class, that William had been picked for the rugby team.

Secretly, William really enjoyed it - it was great to have friends who absolutely believed in you and supported you - but in public he would pretend to be embarrassed by all the praise and attention they were giving him.

By the time Friday came round, William had started to believe his friends and was dreaming he'd be the star player on the team, but then as he was packing his kit after breakfast the realisation hit him - he was going to play in a proper rugby match! He wasn't even sure he knew all the rules, and his dad hadn't been able to help him this week at all.

William had asked a couple of times, but his dad had always been too busy with work. Once his dad had even got changed to come out to the garden with him, but then his phone rang and he sat down to take the call and then had to send more urgent emails. So, other than a bit of messing around with his dad in the garden a few weeks ago and the school trials, he'd never actually played rugby for real.

At school, Tom and Finlay seemed to be even louder and more confident of William's success, but William was quiet for most of the day.

At one point, Tom and Finlay questioned him about it,
"What's up with you, misery guts?" they asked in unison.

"Um... just saving my energy for the match," William lied. That was a mistake though, as it made them both even more confident of his success.

The best thing about being picked for the team was that they had to leave the lesson a bit early, to travel on the bus to Mickleborough School for the match. For William, it meant that not only did he miss some Maths, but he also got the chance to get away from Tom and Finlay who had almost reached fever pitch!

Just as William reached the door to leave the class, Tom shouted out,
"Score a try for us, William!"

The rest of the class giggled and William nipped out of the door as quickly as he could.

As he got on the bus, William recognised some of the other boys from the trials. Of course, Stephen and Harry were there, sitting with all the Year 6 boys acting as though they owned the whole bus. On one of the seats near Stephen and Harry was Simon, he nodded hello to William and William smiled back at him, but he wasn't confident enough to sit near Stephen and Harry and all the Year 6 boys, so he sat at the front.

As they arrived and got off the bus, the Mickleborough team was just leaving the changing room - they looked massive. William gulped and looked at Simon, who had got off the bus next to him. Simon said,

"It's a bigger school than ours, so they're nearly all Year 6 kids. Don't worry though, the bigger they are, the harder they fall!" Then, he grinned and ran into the changing rooms.

Just before they started to get changed Mr Giles came into the room with the players' shirts.

"Right lads, this isn't a cup game, so it's mainly about getting you used to all playing together. But it doesn't mean we don't aim to win. I know you've seen their team - they're good players... and big lads. But you know what - we can beat them! Those of you that played here last year, remember how close we came to beating them and how upset they were when they thought we might win. They expect to win, so they don't like it if you don't roll over with your legs in the air to be tickled."

The boys laughed.

"Ok, then, Number 1, Ben." Ben stood up to collect his shirt. "No penalties in the scrum. You've got quick hands, so use them."

Mr Giles worked his way through the whole team giving out the shirts and offering a few words of advice for all of them. William sat back and waited; it would be a long time before the Number 19 shirt was handed out.

"Number 13, William." William sat bolt upright. He looked around to check there wasn't another William standing up, then he slowly stood up to receive his shirt.

"But I thought I was sub."

"Aaron can't make it as he's had the 'flu this week, so you're in the team, William. Outside centre - an important position. Hold your position and don't let runners past you - if you see a gap, go for it."

In a daze, William sat back down. Then he realised he needed to put his shorts and boots on quickly to run out with the rest of the team as he hadn't even started getting changed yet.

On the way out to the pitch William caught up with Alex, he had heard Mr Giles call him the inside centre, so he thought it might be something similar to his position of outside centre.

"Hey, Alex, wait up."

"Oh hi, William isn't it? Looking forward to it, should be a good match?"

"Well," William said. "Actually, I've not played a match before, so I'm not sure I know what to do."

"Don't worry about it," Alex said. He was a tall, lanky Year 6 kid with floppy blond hair which normally covered his eyes a bit, but for the match he had wet it down and it was sticking to his head.

"You stand on the outside of me - outside centre. Simple really. I'll be closer to the scrum and when I get the ball, I'll either run or pass it to you. If I run, keep up with me cos I might want to pass it to you later. When you get the ball, you either run with it, or pass it to Pete on the wing. Hopefully, he'll then score a try." He grinned. "When they've got the ball, tackle the Number 13 on their team. Just don't let him get past you. Simple really." And with that Alex ran off to join the rest of the team.

The whole team gathered in front of one set of posts and did a quick warm-up. Mr Giles passed the ball to different players and they had to pass it on to someone different. William wasn't quite sure what was going on, but he caught the ball a few times and then passed it to either Simon or Alex. After the passing, they all did a few stretches, under Mr Giles' instructions.

Once the match started, William did as he was told and while he didn't get the ball very often, when Alex did pass it to him, he made sure he passed it on to Pete as quickly as possible. Once he couldn't see where Pete was, so he started running forward with the ball in his hand. The next thing he knew he was in a heap on the ground with a Mickleborough player all over him.

The referee said something about releasing the ball and awarded a penalty to Mickleborough. Some of his team moaned, but a couple of players said,

"Good run!" to him as well.

The tackles he had to make hurt almost as much as being tackled, but they seemed to hurt the opposition player a bit too, and for some reason William liked that. Only a couple of times did the opposite Number 13 get past him; both times Alex soon tackled him and brought him down.

By the time the second half started, William found himself starting to enjoy the game. He knew where he needed to stand without checking where Alex was and his tackles were getting better. Although the Mickleborough Number 13 was clearly a Year 6 kid, he still wasn't as big as William's dad and William could definitely tackle him.

Although Mickleborough were obviously a stronger side than Northbrook, there had been some good moments for William's teammates, including a try which William had a small part to play in. He had managed to pass the ball to Pete, the winger, just as he was being tackled. Pete then ran 30 metres and it looked like he might score, but he couldn't get past the last Mickleborough player. Fortunately, Alex had supported him and Pete was able to pass the ball inside to Alex who scored an easy try. Despite that try, it was no surprise that Mickleborough were winning. However, what was a surprise was, with less than ten minutes to go, they were only winning by four points.

Mickleborough had scored three tries so far, but they had only managed to kick one conversion, which meant they had 17 points. Although Northbrook had only scored one try, they had kicked the conversion and had also managed to score two penalties, so they had 13 points. If Northbrook scored just one more try then they would win the match.

"Keep going, lads!" shouted Mr Giles from the touchline. "You're starting to worry 'em. One try and we'll win this."

A couple of minutes later and Northbrook had managed to work the ball down to only a few metres away from the Mickleborough try line. The forwards had done a great job of controlling the ball and now there was another ruck over by the right-hand touchline.

As the ball came out of the ruck, William could see that the Mickleborough team had been busy defending and were now out of position. The Number 13, who should have been marking William, had to cover two positions as they had a man missing. Instead of standing in front of William, he was between William and Pete, the Northbrook winger, which meant William could see a gap to the try line.

Brian was the Northbrook scrum half. He was a short and skinny Year 6 kid. At first glance, he looked about the size of someone from Year 4, then when you got closer to him and saw his muscles and his face you were surprised he was only in Year 6, he almost looked like he needed to start shaving. He got the ball out of the ruck and straight away passed it to Richard, the stand off, who took two paces forward and then passed it to his left, to Alex, who, with one movement, passed it on to William.

This was William's chance. The Mickleborough Number 13 charged towards him, but there was still a gap on William's left-hand side. However, he would have to be quick as Mickleborough had started to recover their defensive shape and the gap was closing.

Suddenly, William remembered the practising he had been doing with his dad. The dummy pass! He went to pass the ball to his right and back to Alex. The Mickleborough Number 13 took half a step towards his left to anticipate the pass, which caused the gap to the try line to open up again. At the last second, William stopped the pass and brought the ball back to his body. The Mickleborough Number 13 already had his body weight moving left and couldn't change direction again. William had done it, the perfect dummy pass.

He took a step forward, the try line and glory were waiting for William...

But the dummy pass had caused the muddy ball to move ever so slightly in William's grasp. His first step was fine, but as he took his second he could feel the ball slip. By his third step he could tell he was holding on to the pointy end of the ball and not the centre. In a panic,

William looked down at the ball just as it shot forward, almost like a bar of soap. He reached forward to grab it, but it made him stumble and soon both William and the ball were on the floor.

He hadn't scored a try - instead he had knocked the ball on.

It had taken less than three seconds, but it felt like a lifetime to William. As he lay on the floor, he could hear his teammates groan. His chance for glory was over.

William's knock-on resulted in a scrum to Mickleborough which they won easily. They cleared the ball back into the Northbrook half and when the final whistle went a couple of minutes later, they were on the verge of scoring their own try.

As the Northbrook players dejectedly walked off the pitch William could hear a couple of the Year 6 forwards moaning.

"That was the best chance we had of beating Mickleborough in years."

"I know! What on earth was that stupid move he was trying to do?"

William got changed in silence.

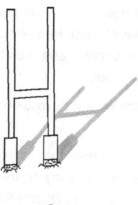

6

"C'mon, misery guts," Tom said to William. "You can't still be sulking about the rugby, can you?"

William just shrugged. It was Tuesday afternoon and Tom and William were walking home together from school; Finlay had left school early to go to the dentist.

It was a bright, sunny day and both boys were just in their shirt sleeves, yet they could tell it was going to be cold later. The sun's rays, which were gently warming the boys' arms as they walked, weren't quite strong enough to fully heat up the day. Every time the boys went into the shade, they shivered slightly.

Or maybe it was just William. The truth was, he *was* still sulking about the rugby. He'd hardly been able to talk to anyone about it since Friday night. In fact, he'd hardly been able to talk about anything since Friday. His mum and dad had tried to ask him about it when he got home, but William just shrugged them off and said he was tired after the match. It was almost a relief to William that they had been so busy arguing this weekend they didn't remember to ask him about it again.

Instead, William had spent most of the weekend replaying the match in his head. The almost perfect dummy pass, just before he dropped the ball and fell over, was like a video on constant repeat.

William hadn't spoken to Tom and Finlay about it either, but they heard enough from the chatter on the playground over the last couple of days. A couple of the Year 6 players were happy to tell everyone about William falling over and how he had lost them the match. Of course, Stephen and Harry were only too quick to join in with these conversations.

There had been lots of jokes in the playground about people dropping things or falling over. Every time William walked past someone, especially if it was a friend of Stephen and Harry, they seemed to have just dropped something.

"Oh no, I've dropped my bag! I hope I don't fall over when I pick it up."

"Careful you don't drop that Stu, you don't want to lose the match."

But Tom and Finlay had heard other stories too. About how William had actually played well. A couple of the other players had said how brave he'd been when tackling the Mickleborough players and how he'd fitted into the team very well - you couldn't tell it was his first game they had said. But every time they'd tried to tell William these reports he'd just changed the subject and walked away.

"Listen, you had a good game and you made one mistake. *You* didn't lose the game, the whole team did," said Tom.

William just shrugged again.

"Oh, suit yourself then." Tom marched ahead on his own. He couldn't deal with William's sulks and wanted to leave him to it.

Just ahead, Tom saw a stick on the ground and picked it up. Actually it wasn't a stick, it was a fallen light sabre, and he wasn't Tom, but Kylo Ren.

"Prepare to meet your doom!" Kylo Ren said to William and poked him with the light sabre. William ignored it, but Kylo Ren started using the light sabre to tickle him. William ran ahead and saw another stick on the ground.

Soon, Luke Skywalker returned with his own light sabre drawn and started to fight Kylo Ren. They fought all the way home until William, who had cheered up and was feeling back to his normal self, waved goodbye to Tom.

The rest of the week had been better, mainly thanks to Tom and Finlay who had made an extra special effort to make William laugh this week and had tried to make sure William didn't hear any of the nastier comments from Stephen and Harry's friends.

But despite all their efforts, William still hadn't been able to face rugby practice this week. So it had come as a shock to him when, as they were dishing up the Chinese takeaway, his dad had asked him about it.

William had to pretend he hadn't heard at first,
"What?"

"I was asking about rugby practice. How was it?" William mumbled a reply as he put a prawn cracker in his mouth, hoping it would satisfy his dad.

"What was that? Finish your mouthful and tell me again." William hadn't gotten away with it.

"I didn't go."

"What? Why not, I thought you loved rugby?"

"Well... It's just... I mean... I dunno, but...," William stammered and he was surprised to feel the tears welling up in his eyes.

William could see his parents exchange a look and then his dad looked at him and said, "Don't worry, Champ, rugby's not going anywhere. Let's eat now." He ruffled William's hair, carried a couple of plates to the table, sat down and started to steal some cashew nuts off William's plate, until William saw what he was up to, laughed and sat down next to him.

As they were clearing away the plates, William's dad looked out of the kitchen window and said, "It's still lovely and sunny outside. Let's get the rugby ball out for ten minutes."

"I dunno Dad, I don't feel like it."

"Go on, William, you'll enjoy it," said his mum. "I'll watch you both while I clear up."

At first, William wasn't very enthusiastic and didn't put much effort in. However, when his dad theatrically dropped the ball for the third time William couldn't help but to laugh. It cheered him up a bit and they started passing it to each other and even practised some pretend line outs. William found himself enjoying rugby again.

"Right then, let's practise the dummy pass again."

Suddenly, William stopped smiling and he could feel the sharp, cold wind blow around the back garden.

"Maybe another day, Dad."

"Ah nonsense," his dad said and all of a sudden, he was next to William showing how to stand and moving his arms for him while they practised dummy passes. When his dad dropped his hands out of the way, William kept going and it started to feel natural to him. He didn't drop the ball. He didn't fall over.

"That's really good, little man. I think you've got the hang of that. But it's gonna start getting dark soon, so let's go in now."

"I'll just be a few more minutes, Dad, I want to practise a little more," William replied.

"Okay, I'll give you a shout in ten minutes," his dad said as he received one last pass from William, did his own dummy pass, passed it back to William and then went inside.

William carried on practising the dummy pass, but after a few minutes he wanted to add an extra dimension to it. He threw the ball up in the air and caught it, to make it feel like he was receiving a pass from another player. Then he did a dummy pass, before taking a couple of steps forward. This made it harder, but he was still enjoying it and practising hard.

He threw the ball a bit higher this time and just as he was about to catch it,

"William!" his dad shouted from the top of the garden. William took his eye off the ball, it hit him on the chin and bounced on the ground.

"Ow." He looked around and the ball had disappeared.

"I'll just be a couple more minutes, Dad," he called out.

"Two more and then that's it."

"Ok."

The back garden had three different levels. At the top, right next to the house was a small patio where William's mum and dad would sometimes sit out with a glass of wine. Occasionally, all three of them would eat out there. After the patio, the garden started to slope slightly downhill and his parents had planted flowers in that section. Then finally, at the bottom, there was a green, square section of lawn, with a border of tall bushes and trees.

When William was young, the lawn had seemed huge. He remembered running races round the grass - 'the 'Lympics' he used to call it - but after three laps he would be exhausted. It didn't seem quite so big now, but it was a good place to practise his rugby, apart from when he lost the ball.

After the ball had hit him in the face, it had bounced towards the thick bushes at the edge of the grass; they seemed to have swallowed the ball completely. There was no sign of it at all.

William looked down and tried to follow a route from his chin, which the ball had bounced off, towards the bushes, to see where the ball may have entered. He got down on his hands and knees and crawled into the shrubs.

It was amazing how thick all the different stalks, trunks and leaves of the bushes were once you were inside, but he could just see the ball up ahead. One of the bushes seemed to be made up of red sticks and the ball was lying just at the foot of it. William stretched out, gathered up the ball and carefully crawled out backwards.

"Thanks for getting the ball back, Billy. But get yourself warm, we might need you on soon."

William almost jumped out of his skin with surprise. He couldn't see who had spoken, but he knew it wasn't his dad's voice. This voice was deeper and cracklier and on top of that, he'd called him 'Billy'; no-one shortened his name like that. And what did he mean about 'getting warm'?

He continued crawling out of the bushes and stood up to face the mysterious voice, but as he turned round, the owner of the voice became the least mysterious thing he had to worry about. William's mind was now racing and trying to work out firstly, why it was daylight again, and secondly, who had put a rugby pitch in his back garden. Although when he looked again, he wasn't even sure it was his back garden, as he could no longer see his house.

While he was trying to process all of this a deep voice shouted out,

"Pass it then!"

He looked over and saw a much older boy, who looked like he might be one of Tom's older brother's friends. William passed the ball, but even this surprised him as he was able to throw it harder and faster than he ever had before. William looked at his hands and they seemed different: bigger and stronger somehow.

In all of the confusion William didn't realise the ball had been thrown back to him and it hit his chest and fell to the ground.

"C'mon, Billy. Wake up!"

William jogged over to the edge of the car park - Wait a minute, a car park! - as the ball had rolled close to one of the parked cars. Reflected in the back window of the car was the face of someone much older, someone maybe 19 or 20 years old. William looked around in surprise, ready to hand the ball back to him. But there was no-one there. Slowly he put his hand to his face and the hand of the reflection did the same. He touched his nose, then ran his fingers through his hair - the reflection did the same. What was going on?

"Alright, gorgeous. Stop admiring yourself!" came the shout from one of the other players and William realised there were four of them, all wearing rugby kit with a red tracksuit top over their shirts. William looked down and realised he was wearing the same kit.

"Stop chatting, you lot, and get warmed up. Billy, Stuart, you're going to be on in two minutes."

The other boys stopped laughing and started to jog round the pitch. William caught up with them, still confused, and followed their warm-up routine of stretches, side-to-side running and even a few sprints.

The man with the deep, crackly voice looked like the coach and he was soon waving to William to come over to him.

"Right, tracksuit off, Billy. You're going on. I know this is your first game for the second team, but all you need to do is what you've been doing in training. You're a natural outside centre. Use your quick hands, your strength and if you spot a gap, use your pace too. On you go."

He gave William a push in the back and before he knew it William was jogging onto the rugby pitch.

The team in red clapped and a couple of the players shouted words of encouragement,

"C'mon, Billy", "Yay, Billy the Kid". William looked down as he ran on and he was wearing a red top too, so he joined their side.

William didn't have time to work out what was going on as the match started around him so quickly. It was similar to the match he'd played for the school team, but everything was faster and all the players stronger. William was tackled a couple of times and they felt bigger and harder than he was used to, but they didn't hurt William as he too was bigger and stronger.

The game was over within a few minutes and William soon realised he'd only been on the pitch for the last ten minutes. As the players came off, the coach came up to him and patted him on the back,

"A good run out there, Billy. Well done, lad."

William followed the rest of the team into the changing rooms and had a shower with them. He didn't know where his clothes were at first, but then he recognised the same boot bag he took to school. It was one his dad had bought for him when he'd been away on a work trip. It had 'Barcelona' written on it.

There were lots of jokes and laughter in the changing rooms and the older boys were using a lot of rude words too. William sat quietly and got changed into the strange clothes on the peg. He was amazed when the trainers, which were a size 11, fitted him perfectly, and the jeans, which seemed massive when he'd taken them off the peg, were actually a bit tight.

As they were leaving, two or three of the older players smiled and waved at him, "Well played there, Billy." William smiled and followed them out of the changing rooms. As he stepped out of the building he looked around and the sun shone directly into his eyes. William closed his eyes for a moment to stop the sunlight blinding him.

$$O \quad O \quad O$$

"There you are!" Suddenly, William was back in the garden and it was his dad's voice he could hear. "I said come in before it got dark. I almost needed one of these to find you," he said, waving a torch into William's eyes.

"Erm, but..." William looked around and he was in his back garden again, the rugby ball was in his hands and he was wearing the same scruffy trousers he'd put on after tea.

He looked up at his dad and tried to explain what had just happened. But as William opened his mouth he realised that not only would his dad not believe it, he wasn't sure if he believed it either. His dad was just looking at him, waving the torch and waiting for a response from William.

"Yeah," he said. "Sorry about that," and they went inside together.

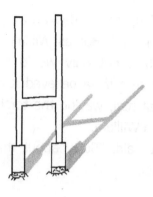

7

William didn't sleep well that night. He couldn't stop replaying the rugby match he had been part of. Or had he? It certainly wasn't William as he was now - that player was all grown up - but it felt like him. He remembered the feel of the ball in his hand, the sunshine on his skin and the wind blowing through his hair. He even remembered the force of the tackles the opposition made. In fact, just thinking about it made William rub his leg again where one of the hardest tackles had hit him.

"Ow!"

The pain was sharp. He yelled out and was worried he might have woken up his mum and dad, as he felt a bruise.

William sat up in bed and turned on his night-light. He tried to roll his pyjama leg up to see the bruise, but he couldn't get it high enough. Instead he had to pull his trousers down a little to look. And there was a huge, purple bruise just below his hip, on the top of his left thigh.

He remembered the tackle. He'd only been playing for a couple of minutes and he had barely touched the ball. There was a ruck in the middle of the pitch, William's team had time to set themselves into an attacking formation and they had split the backs, so that half were on the left and half on the right, behind the ruck. William was on the right and the scrum half passed the ball straight to him. For a split-second William didn't know what to do next and he froze - that was all it took.

He didn't see the tackle coming. Maybe this was why it hurt so much. Or maybe it was because the tackler was a man as old as his dad, but much bigger and stronger. He was a forward who had broken off from the ruck as soon as the ball was passed. He went straight for William and by the time William had reacted to receiving the ball, there he was. William had turned to his right to see who he should pass to which was why he didn't see the tackle coming. But he certainly felt it.

In bed, William winced at the thought of it. The man was huge. He was at least a couple of inches taller than William's dad and a lot heavier. He wasn't fat exactly, but nor did he look like he was super muscly. He was just bigger and stronger and he knew how to tackle. Hard.

65

But then William thought about it a bit more. If he, William the schoolboy, had been tackled by a man like that he would have been crushed, and although his bruise hurt, that's all it was. Well, that and another bruise on his shoulder where he fell down. But only bruises, no broken bones.

He hadn't been crushed. So maybe it wasn't William the schoolboy who had been playing rugby. Everyone had been calling him Billy, so maybe he really had been Billy after all. But who was Billy?

$$\mathcal{O} \quad \mathcal{O} \quad \mathcal{O}$$

During lunchtime break the following day, William asked Tom and Finlay,

"Have you ever had weird dreams which feel real?"

"What now?" Tom asked. "Have you been dreaming about kissing Abigail and woken up kissing the pillow?" Both Tom and Finlay laughed at the joke.

Abigail had dark skin, long dark hair and big brown eyes. She sat at the front of the class and always put her hand up whenever Miss Heath asked a question. When William had first joined the school, he hadn't been able to stop staring at Abigail, but he'd never actually managed to talk to her. He'd only tried once and she had walked right past him as if he wasn't there. Tom had laughed about it for nearly three whole days.

"Stop it!" William said. "I don't even like her. No, it must have been a dream; it felt like it was real, but it can't have been."

"Do you mean it was like a vision or a hallucination?" asked Finlay. "I think I read something about hallucinations putting real memories in people's brains, even though the hallucination itself was obviously not real. Do you think it might have been something like that?"

"Maybe. It was just, oh I don't know. I mean it can't have been real," William's voice trailed away as he was lost in his memories. He touched his leg and winced as he felt the bruise again.

Tom looked at Finlay and they both shrugged. William had been weird all week, maybe it was the rugby match that was still bothering him. Whatever it was, they hoped he would snap out of it soon.

Wednesday was the day the rugby team was usually announced for the match on Friday, so after the final bell rang, instead of just rushing out of school and walking home together, Tom, Finlay and William walked round to the school office to look at the notice board.

There were a number of other kids hanging round, most of them were from Year 6 and they were blocking the board for everyone else. William decided to wait at the back of the group until things cleared.

Unfortunately, though, being at the back meant he was easier to spot by Stephen and Harry as they arrived to look at the team list. Suddenly, from nowhere, William got shoved in the back as Harry banged into him.

The shove caused William to drop his school bag, which of course meant Stephen laughed at him and said something about William always dropping things.

William could feel the tears welling up in his eyes and he just wanted to run away. He had to pick up his bag first, so he bent down to get it and as he did Harry nudged him just enough to make William lose balance and fall over. Both Stephen and Harry laughed and walked towards William on the floor.

"Hey, William! You doing okay?"

It was a Year 6 kid. William didn't recognise him at all. How did he know William?

"Erm, yeah I'm fine thanks," William mumbled, still on the floor. Then, suddenly it came to him. "How are you, Ben?" It was his rugby teammate from last week.

Ben didn't answer, he just grinned and gave him a thumbs up as he walked off with his friends. However, the fact Ben had spoken to him had caused Stephen and Harry to back away and so William had been able to get back to his feet and pick his bag up. As the crowd moved away, William saw his chance to have a look at the teamsheet.

He looked straight for the Number 13 position, to see if he would be playing next to Alex again. However, it wasn't William's name written there, but 'Jasper Evans' instead. William didn't even know who Jasper was, maybe he was another Year 6 player. Before he looked down to the list of substitutes William could see that Alex was still playing at Number 12.

There were five substitutes listed: Conrad Smith, Adam Wilkinson, Simon Johnson, Andrew Dawson and Ranjit Patel. William looked up and down the list again, but his name definitely wasn't there. His heart sank.

Further down the corridor, Tom and Finlay were being hassled by Stephen and Harry now. They had taken Finlay's bag and were throwing it to each other so that it was passing over Tom and Finlay's heads. Tom was trying to jump up to catch it, but Finlay was just ignoring them. However, Tom saw William's shoulders slump, so he stopped jumping and came and stood next to William.

"I've not been picked," William said.

"Are you sure?" asked Tom and he repeated William's routine of looking at the Number 13 and then reading the names of the substitutes. "Well, maybe you've picked in another position." Tom read through the entire team from 1 to 15 and then back again just in case he'd missed anything.

He hadn't.

"Hey never mind, buddy, there are a lot more matches left this year. I'm sure you'll be picked again."

"Oh no, poor William. Did you get dropped?" laughed Stephen from down the corridor.

"A bit like the rugby ball whenever you get it," jeered Harry and he threw Finlay's bag at him and the two of them walked off.

"Ignore them," said Finlay. "Come on, let's go home."

William didn't say much as they were walking home, so Tom and Finlay left him to his thoughts.

"I didn't even realise I liked rugby this much until the first match," said William, as much to himself as to the other two. "I mean, I know I wasn't much good, but I absolutely want to play again. I'm sure I can get the dummy pass right if I keep going."

"I'm pretty sure that Jasper Evans is in Year 6 and I think he's good friends with Alex, maybe that's why he got picked this week," said Finlay.

"Hey, maybe he'll drop the ball too," said Tom. "I mean, you know..." But Finlay gave him an evil look and Tom stopped talking.

"Sorry, mate, I didn't mean that," said Tom. "But you know, I bet he's not actually that good and you'll play next week."

"It's true," said Finlay. "Mr Giles is still trying to work out what his best team is. The cup matches don't start until next week, so this is just a friendly and he's trying lots of different players. I'm sure you'll get picked again when the important matches start."

"Yeah, maybe," William said glumly.

He was still upset about the rugby, but it did make him feel a lot better to have friends like these two. They were always trying to support him and he appreciated that.

They walked on in silence until they got to Finlay's house and saw William's mum waiting at the edge of the churchyard.

"Hello, boys," William's mum called out and smiled. She gently put her arm around William's shoulder, but was talking to all three of them.

"How was school today?"

"Yeah, it was alright," William mumbled in reply.

"He didn't get picked for the rugby team, so he's sulking a bit," Tom said. William shot him a look and stormed off.

"Oh no!" his mum said. "Thanks for telling me, Tom. I'd better go and see if he's ok." She rushed off to follow William.

"What did you say that for?" asked Finlay. "He wasn't sulking, he was just a bit upset about it."

"Whatever. That looked like a sulk to me," said Tom and off he went kicking a stone down the road.

By the time William's mum had caught up to him, he'd wiped the tears from his eyes.

"Are you alright, love?" she asked him.

"I'm not sulking, I'm just..." But the tears were in his eyes again. William's mum pulled him into her and he started to cry into her jumper. Within a few seconds though he pulled away, wiped his eyes and stood up straight.

"Rugby players don't cry," he said. "And that's what I want to be."

71

"It's ok to cry you know, darling. You're allowed to be upset about it. You liked playing in the first match and you want to play again."

"I'm not upset. I'm just... I'm frustrated. I know I wasn't any good, but I really wanted to play again this week."

"There are plenty more matches and I'm sure you'll play again soon, my wonderful, determined boy," said his mum as she hugged him again.

o o o

"Can I go out and play please, Mum?"

"I'm not sure I've ever seen you eat so quickly," his mum replied. "What are you in a rush for?"

"I just want to practise my rugby. I want to be so good that Mr Giles will never drop me again." Overnight, it had occurred to William he hadn't been chosen as he hadn't gone to rugby practice. Dad always told him how important it was to practise.

His mum laughed,

"Okay then, off you go. You've got 45 minutes before I call you in to get ready for bed. And don't give yourself indigestion after eating so quickly."

William rushed out and picked up his rugby ball as he went. He ran down to the bottom of the garden and practised a few dummy passes.

He did want to practise, but it wasn't the main reason for being there. He threw the ball around for a couple of minutes and waved at his mum who was looking out of

72

the kitchen window at him, then he accidentally dropped the ball near the plant with the strange red stalks and started looking for the mysterious secret hole. What William actually wanted to do was to see if he could find the adult match again. He wanted to find out who Billy was and to see if he could join in with another match.

He searched next to the plant, but couldn't see anything different. He tried crawling through the hedge and back again two or three times, but each time he came back into his own garden.

"What are you doing, Champ?" It was his dad who had come back home earlier than usual and had seen William in the garden. "Are you practising? Shall I throw you a few passes?"

"Erm, yeah, okay." William wasn't sure how to explain to his dad what he was really doing, so they threw a few passes to each other.

His dad stood in the middle of the garden and the routine they created was one where William would slowly run around the outside edge of the lawn, receive a pass from his dad, practise a dummy pass, then pass it back again. Once he'd run all the way around his dad he turned round and did it in the opposite direction, so William could practise with both hands.

William loved playing with his dad like this, but his mind was now occupied with trying to find the strange portal which had taken him into the other match last night. He didn't know if he'd be able to with his dad around. Would his dad be able to follow him in? And how old would he be if he did? Or would William just disappear into thin air and leave his dad on his own in the garden?

He didn't know the answer to any of those questions, and he was a little bit nervous about what might happen, but it didn't stop him trying.

William didn't want to make it obvious to his dad what he was doing, so he developed a sneaky plan. Every second time he received a pass near the plant with the red stalks, he missed the ball and let it bounce into the bushes.

"I'll get it," he'd shout and dive into the bushes to look for the hole. Sometimes he nudged the rugby ball further into the bushes with his knee as he got down to crawl, meaning he had to wriggle even further in. Once he even passed it the wrong way and threw it deep into the hedge instead of passing it to his dad.

His dad was getting a bit frustrated with William dropping the ball so much, and with him taking so long to pick it up again.

"Come on, concentrate! Watch the ball, all the way into your hands! It can't take that long to pick it up. It's right there, pick it up and let's carry on!"

William felt a bit guilty deceiving his dad in this way, but it was worth it to have a good look for the magic hole. The frustrating part was that he couldn't find it. He looked everywhere. He was sure he was in the right spot, but every time he picked up the ball and stood up he was still in his own garden, practising with his own dad.

The practice with his dad was good, but it wasn't anywhere near as good as playing a real match as Billy.

He'd dropped the ball about fifteen times when he heard his mum shout,

"Boys! Time for William to come in now."

"Okay," his dad shouted back. "We'll just be two more minutes."

"Right then," he said as he turned to William. "Two more laps, one in each direction and then we'll go in. And concentrate on every pass; let's do both laps without dropping the ball once."

William nodded and off they went. The first throw from his dad was a little bit too far in front of him, so he had to reach out to catch it, but he did, executed a great dummy pass to his left and turned back to his dad and passed it straight to him.

"Great stuff!" his dad said as he caught the ball. "And again," as he threw it again for William. This time the ball was a bit behind William and he had to stop running to catch it, but he did and did another dummy pass before he returned it to his dad.

His dad was a bit more accurate with the next two passes and William caught them well, did the dummy pass and returned the ball right into his dad's hands.

"Well done! Now the other way," his dad said.

William turned round and went round the garden in the other direction. This time his dad was on his left, so he caught the ball with his left hand below and in front of his right hand, pretended to pass the ball to his right, took another step forward, then passed the ball back to his dad on the left.

The first three went well. William caught the ball cleanly, perfectly executed the dummy pass and then on the fourth one William dropped the ball.

"William!" his dad scolded. "Come on, concentrate!" Then his tone softened slightly, "You've done some great catches and passes tonight, don't let a lack of concentration let you down. Right then, time to go in."

But William wasn't listening. Although this dropped pass really was an accident it had happened right in front of the plant with the red stalks. He had one last chance to find the portal, one last chance to find out more about Billy, one last chance to play an adult game of rugby again.

"William! Are you listening? Come on, it's time for us to go in." His dad took a step towards where William was kneeling, on the edge of the plants. William had bent down to pick up the ball, but had accidentally knocked it further away from him and towards the red stalks.

"Sorry, Dad, be with you in a minute."

"Well hurry up. It's nearly your bedtime and with all that crawling around you need a shower tonight."

"Ok, I'll be there in just a minute," William called from deep within the bushes.

His dad walked back to the house and as he did William crawled deeper in. He knew he'd annoyed his dad tonight and he'd only have a few minutes before his dad told him to come in again, but he just had to have another look.

When William's dad got to the back door he carefully took off his muddy shoes - he'd need to give them a good clean, but not tonight, he was too tired. It would probably be good to let all the mud dry anyway, then they'd be easier to clean. Even with his shoes off he was in danger of leaving a trail of mud everywhere as the bottom of each trouser leg was muddy. So, he rolled each trouser leg up before stepping into the house and onto the carpet.

He went upstairs to change and after a few minutes he came back downstairs with a clean pair of trousers and his slippers on. As he walked into the kitchen, he saw William's mum staring out of the kitchen window, she'd been washing up, but now just stood there with soapy hands staring.

"What's he doing, Mark?" she asked and pointed out to the garden.

"Eh?" William's dad followed her hand and saw William still kneeling in the bushes.

"Right, that's it. I told him to come in. I'm going to get him." And he marched angrily across the kitchen towards the back door.

"Wait! Just come and look at this though. He's been doing it for five minutes now and I can't work out why."

William's mum turned to face her husband.

"Should we be worried?" she said, with tears starting to fill her eyes.

William's dad stopped and looked out again.

"He was doing that while we played. I just thought he was messing around."

As they both stood there William had one last look around. He went to the right-hand side of the plant with the red stalks, then to the left. Then he tried to go backwards to the right and again backwards to the left. Finally, he crawled around the back and right round in a circle. It was no good, he couldn't find the hole. Maybe it was just a dream. Maybe he'd never find out any more about Billy. He squatted down on his knees and sighed. Tears started to flow and he sniffed, trying to hold them back.

Through the tears he could see his mum and dad looking out of the window and he realised he'd be in trouble for not going in quickly enough. He picked up the rugby ball, waved up at the window and stood up out of the bushes, stepped onto the grass and ran as quickly as he could up to the back door.

As he stepped inside the door, he was waiting to be told off, so he steeled himself for it. Instead, his mum tenderly kissed him on the forehead and asked him if he was alright. That was too much for William and he broke down into floods of tears. He couldn't explain what was wrong, but neither could he stop the tears. He cried all the way through his shower, cried while he was brushing his teeth and cried even more when his parents kissed him goodnight.

His mum pulled his bedroom door to, making sure she left it open enough so the light at the top of the stairs shone slightly into William's room. William finally stopped crying. All the rugby and crying had worn him out and he fell asleep before his mum had carefully tiptoed all the way down to the bottom step of the stairs. He dreamt of rugby, of dummy passes ... and of Billy.

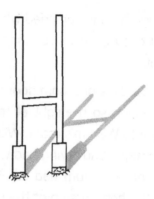

8

During the next couple of days at school, William was quiet and didn't say a lot. Tom and Finlay had learned not to question him when he was in this mood, so they stayed quiet too. During break times, the three of them just sat on the edge of the playground and talked in detail about the relative strengths of the characters on the cards they were collecting.

"There's no way your lasers would ever hit my guy, not with his super speed. My guy would be out of there before your lasers even warmed up."

"But your speed's no good if the anti-gravity force field is on. No-one can run around while that's on."

"My rockets would just destroy any force field."

"Not if my lasers had already destroyed your rockets."

On Thursday lunchtime they started to be bothered by Stephen and Harry - "How about if my giant hand destroyed all your rockets?" said Stephen as he knocked all of Tom's cards out of his hand.

"Oi, that's not fair!" Tom yelled as he started to scramble around to pick up his cards. "Why do you have to ruin everything?"

It might have got much worse if at that moment Alex hadn't walked over to William.

"Hiya, Will. Are you playing tomorrow?"

"Er, no. I wasn't picked this week."

"Oh, that's a shame. I thought you played really well the other day. What's that you've got? Oh, I love those cards."

Slowly, Stephen and Harry walked away and left them to it. As they walked away looking for someone else they could pick on, they heard Alex say,

"How about if we had rugby cards, what would your strengths be?"

William was also unusually quiet at home. On Thursday, he had to complete his maths homework - twenty long division examples to work through before the test on Friday - so he sat at the dining table and finished his homework before tea.

He and his mum then had their tea together - fish fingers and chips, with peas. William was allowed to have one of his favourite yoghurts - the ones in a tube - for his dessert and then he had time for half an hour of television before it was bedtime.

He was watching the TV when his dad came home. "Hey, William. How are you, Champ?"

William just grunted and waved because the programme was getting to the good bit - the aliens had discovered the source of the vampires' power and they were planning their attack on it.

William's dad walked into the kitchen and spoke to his mum as she was clearing their tea things away. Their conversation didn't sound very friendly, so William just turned the TV up a bit louder. When he was younger, they would kiss each other all the time - in front of William and his friends too, it was super embarrassing - but now he missed those days.

Nowadays, there weren't many kisses. Instead, his parents regularly had the kind of conversation which sounded like they were shouting at each other, but in a whisper. Once or twice, when William had gone to bed, they forgot the whisper bit and they just shouted. William would wake up and sometimes he'd just lie in bed listening. Even when they were shouting though, they didn't sound angry, not like they used to when they used to frighten William; or when William shouted at Tom, who could be really annoying at times. No, his parents sounded, well, William could only describe it as sad and disappointed

On those nights when William woke up, he sometimes wondered if he was to blame, if he made them sad. He knew deep down this was one of the reasons why he wanted to be a great rugby player, to make them happy. But he wasn't sure if even that would be enough.

He'd spoken to Tom and Finlay about it, but only once.

"Do your parents ever row with each other?" he'd asked.

Tom laughed,

"The other day my dad came into the kitchen after fixing the chain on my bike. His hands were covered in oil, the back of his trousers were too where he'd wiped his hands. He sat down on the kitchen chair, you know, the new ones they'd just bought. You should have heard my mum shout at him. In fact, I'm surprised you didn't hear my mum shout at him."

William and Finlay laughed. They'd heard Tom's mum shout, especially when Tom walked into the house with dirty shoes, which he did all the time.

"No, I don't mean like that. I mean a proper row. Your mum and dad obviously like each other, even if your mum does shout. Sometimes I'm not sure my parents like each other very much anymore," said William.

"I don't remember whether my parents used to row," said Finlay, "but I heard my mum read from one of her magazines once. It said that couples need to have a shared hobby and that they shouldn't stay together for the children's sake, or something like that. It also said that a good row can be healthy."

"Maybe having rows is your parents' hobby," laughed Tom as he ran off down the road. William and Finlay followed him and William never mentioned it to them again.

Tonight his parents had remembered to keep their shouting to a whisper and so he could only hear a few words through the sound of the television - "...always late home..., I do have a job to do you know..., what about my work?..., little team of two..., I couldn't keep it warm if I didn't know when you'd be back..., just some respect..., it goes both ways..."

"Right, Champ, bedtime." This time the voice was loud and clear and coming from the doorway of the front room, not through the wall of the kitchen. It was William's dad.

"Yeah, in a minute," William mumbled. He was now watching another programme about a team of kids who solved mysteries.

"Now!" came the sharp reply. "You know the rules."

William jumped off the sofa, he could tell by his dad's tone it wasn't worth arguing with him, so he ran straight upstairs to put his pyjamas on. He wondered if he'd be woken up again tonight, but he soon fell fast asleep.

The next morning over breakfast, his parents weren't arguing, so William ate his Cheerios and read the back of the box. Almost as soon as he started, his dad stood up, left the table and went back upstairs. He was back down within a couple of minutes and kissed William on the top of the head.

84

"See you, Champ, have a great day. Love you."

"Love you too, Dad."

"What time will you be back tonight, Mark?" his mum asked sharply.

"Oh, don't start all that again," sighed his dad and he stepped out of the door and got into the car. William and his mum could hear the car pull off the drive and go down the road.

As he walked into school with Tom and Finlay, William noticed a few of the Year 6 boys with their sports bags. Of course, the rugby team had a match tonight. The rugby team, which didn't include him, had a match tonight. This put William in an even worse mood.

The school day passed by quickly and quietly for William. He managed to laugh in the drama class when Miss Heath had dressed Tom up as a woman to demonstrate how boys always took the female parts in Shakespeare's time. Tom quite enjoyed himself for a while and even started to do an impression of Miss Heath herself until she realised what he was doing and told him off. The whole class tried very hard not to laugh, but not many of them managed it. It took Miss Heath at least ten minutes to calm everyone down and it was only when Tom returned from getting changed again the class became quiet.

Other than that, William stayed quiet for the day. Every time he started to cheer up a bit he'd see one of the Year 6 rugby players and his mood would plummet.

"Come on then, sulk chops," said Tom as they were clearing away the art supplies. "Just one more lesson and then you can go home and be moody."

William looked up, but Tom wasn't angry with him. Tom smiled, patted him on the back and then walked over to his table and got his Maths book out ready. William finished putting the coloured paper back in the drawer and sat down next to Tom at his desk. He took his Maths book out and realised it would soon be the weekend and this horrible week would be over.

As soon as he got in through the front door, William dumped his school bag and ran upstairs to get changed. Normally, he stayed in his school uniform until it was bedtime, but today he wanted to take it off as soon as he could. He came back downstairs a few minutes later in his favourite old jeans and a t-shirt and he instantly felt a bit better.

His mum was waiting for him at the bottom of the stairs and she just pointed at his school bag.

"Come on," she chided. "You know it doesn't go there. And what about your homework, have you got any to do over the weekend?"

William mumbled something about 'maths' as he moved his bag and put it in the cupboard under the stairs where it belonged. Then he slumped on the sofa and turned the TV on.

"Are you alright?" his mum asked. William nodded without turning round and his mum knew better than to push things. He could have a couple of hours in front of the TV if that's what he needed.

William wasn't even sure what he was watching, but it passed the time and meant he didn't have to think about rugby. After about two hours of cartoons, his dad came through the door with the Chinese takeaway. William turned off the TV and got ready to steal a prawn cracker or two.

"Hello. I'm home. Fiona, Will, the Chinese is here." William's dad dumped the food in the kitchen and went up the stairs to get changed.

William wasn't sure where his mum was, so he opened the bag of prawn crackers straight away and took one out. He was just reaching in for his second one when his mum came into the kitchen.

"Hey, I saw that!" she said, but she was smiling at William and nodded as he held the prawn cracker up to his mouth. As he ate it, William helped his mum to unpack all the food.

"Hang on a minute," she said, more to herself than William and she looked through all the food again. William heard a loud tut and his mum walked out of the kitchen.

"Mark, did you get my message?" she yelled up the stairs. "Or did you just not think? Or do you just not care?" His dad appeared at the top of the stairs with his shirt off and a towel over his shoulder.

"What's wrong now, Fiona? Can't you just give me a minute of peace to get changed?"

Another tut from William's mum and she marched back into the kitchen. Plates were banged onto the table and knives and forks were slammed down next to them.

"Are you ok, Mum? Can I help with anything?"

"Get yourself a drink and just sit down," she snapped back and then seeing William's face she took another prawn cracker and offered it to him and ruffled his hair as he sat down.

At that moment, William's dad walked into the kitchen. He had changed out of his suit and was wearing his usual Friday night jeans and the sweatshirt with the holes in it.

"Right then, what's all the drama about?"

"Drama! Drama? I suppose I'm overreacting to this as well, am I?"

"What on earth is this about?" shouted William's dad, shocking William and his mum.

"Don't shout at me! Where's my pork? Did you not get my message? It was a simple request."

William's dad's face crumpled,

"Oh, no! I'm really sorry. I completely forgot."

"Like you always seem to do. If it's work you always remember. When it comes to me and William, maybe we're not so important."

"Oh, that's not fair. Look, I had a really busy day..."

88

"The same excuse every time. It's just not good enough Mark."

William's dad started to dish the food out, "Look, it's not as if you don't like this is it? I mean you normally love the beef."

"It was a simple request, that's all. I'd just like you to put us first once in a while," but the anger in her voice was now replaced by resignation. She poured out two glasses of wine and topped up William's glass of water. They both took a prawn cracker and then William's dad put down their plates in front of them. He sat down with his food and they all started to eat.

There wasn't as much chat around the table as on a normal Friday, in fact they ate in almost complete silence. William wasn't very hungry and pushed the food around on his plate more than he put it into his mouth. After a few more minutes, and after only about three more mouthfuls of food, he stood up.

"I'm done," he said as he took his still half-full plate over to the sink. Normally, he would have been told to sit down and finish what was on his plate, but instead his mum just said, "Ok," and topped up her wine.

William slumped in front of the TV again but couldn't sit still and he certainly couldn't concentrate on the cartoon. He could almost feel the silence and the tension from the kitchen pressing down on him, so he put his shoes on and picked up his rugby ball.

Walking through the kitchen, he grabbed a couple more prawn crackers and mumbled,

"I'll be in the garden."

He didn't even wait to hear the non-reply as he shut the back door behind him.

Walking down to the bottom of the garden he had to concentrate to keep the tears back. He hated it when his parents were like this and it was happening more and more often. As he reached the lawn area, he dropped his rugby ball to the floor and sat down on it, trying to work out if there was anything he could do to make things better between them.

He didn't understand what the problem was; he just knew there were more moods and less laughing than there used to be. Maybe he should do something to make them laugh and that would help. But he couldn't think of anything.

By now the silence in the kitchen had spread to the rest of the house as William's dad had taken his full glass of wine upstairs and his mum had topped up her own glass and started to clear the table.

"You relax after your hard day at work, I'll tidy everything up," she muttered sarcastically under her breath.

William's dad put the glass of wine down on the windowsill in his office,

"I just forgot," he sighed and he stared out of the window.

Outside, William stood up and picked up the ball. He wasn't sure he felt like playing rugby, but being outside was better than being in there, with them. He dropped the ball and pretended to do a drop kick – which is kicking the ball just as it bounces. He intended to miss it completely, but caught the ball with the very outside of his foot and it shot away from him and into the bushes. In the fading light he couldn't quite see where it had gone.

"Great! Just what I need!" he said to himself as he knelt down to try and find it.

$\bigcirc$ $\bigcirc$ $\bigcirc$

"Come on, leave the ball alone, Billy!" came the shout from his left. "We're gonna make you put in some hard fitness training first," and then the voice broke into a laugh.

William stood up, but he was no longer in his back garden, instead he was on the edge of a floodlit rugby pitch with 30 or 40 players all walking around and nervously chatting to each other. He looked down and could see he was wearing rugby boots, a pair of tight leggings with shorts over the top of them, a red rugby shirt and a hoodie.

"Hurry up, Billy. Join in!"

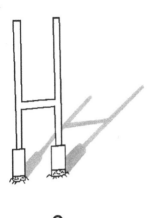

9

As Billy joined the rest of the team, he could hear some of them moaning about 'fitness week'. It seemed whenever they had a weekend without a match, the training session was extra tough, with more running and fitness work than usual.

They started with a gentle jog. Billy assumed they would just jog around the pitch, but instead they ran around the whole field, which had four different pitches on it. Then, they had to run in pairs. This time they just ran around one pitch, but the pair at the back of the group had to sprint forward until they were at the front, then they were able to jog again until every other pair had run past them and they were at the back. From the back, they had to repeat the sprint to the front. They did this until every pair had sprinted forward six times, it took eight laps of the pitch to complete it.

Billy was already exhausted and panting heavily, but he was enjoying feeling fit and strong. Everyone took a short break to catch their breath and to grab a drink.

$$\circ \quad \circ \quad \circ$$

Fiona was sorting out some laundry in the bedroom. She was still annoyed about the takeaway and washing her husband's underpants was about the last thing she wanted to do. She tipped the laundry basket onto the bed and started sorting out a load. Subconsciously, she was prioritising hers and William's clothes and leaving Mark's on the side - they could be washed later.

As she'd come into the bedroom she glanced down at William in the back garden. It was getting dark and it was almost time he should come in, but she was confused to see him just standing there. She watched for a minute, but he didn't seem to be really doing anything. She decided as soon as she'd sorted out the laundry she would call him in.

Once she had a full basket ready for the wash, she picked it up and headed downstairs. She glanced out of the window again to see what William was up to and he certainly wasn't standing around anymore.

He was running, no, actually he was sprinting, all by himself! He was only running forwards and back in their garden, but he was doing it with an intensity and a passion she had never seen before. He would do a couple of sprints and then stop to catch his breath, then off he would go again.

Fiona couldn't put her finger on it, but she could swear while he was catching his breath William was talking to someone and cheering people on. But there was no-one else there... was there?

She couldn't tear her eyes away from the window and her son in the garden below.

$\mathcal{O} \quad \mathcal{O} \quad \mathcal{O}$

Once they'd all had a drink, the players were split up into four teams to do something the coach called 'shuttle sprints'. Teams were organised so they had an equal number of forwards, the big and strong (but not very quick players) and backs, the ones who were expected to sprint during the games. As Billy joined the third team, a couple of the forwards clapped and called him 'a flyer', which Billy assumed meant people expected him to be a quick runner.

All the teams were lined up on the try line and they were going to race. Each person had to sprint to the 5-metre line and back and then run backwards to the 22-metre line and sprint back. Once everyone in the team had done it they all had to go again, but this time sprinting up to the half-way line and back and then again to the 22-metre line and back. Once everyone in the team had done both of those, they were finished; the first team to finish was the winner.

Billy's team started with a couple of forwards and so were soon trailing behind the others, but when it was Billy's turn he realised he was racing against forwards on the other teams and, despite nearly falling over when it came to the backwards running, he soon caught up with them.

When he had finished his first sprints, he cheered on his teammates until it was his turn to go again. The forwards had again got the team off to a slow start, but Billy sprinted hard to the half-way line and back and then again to the 22-metre line and back, so by the time he had finished his sprints his team were in the lead. Unfortunately, the final two runners in the team couldn't keep the lead and Billy's team came second.

Everyone apart from the winning team had to do ten press-ups, which got lots of groans from the players, apart from those on the winning team who jeered and laughed.

$$O \quad O \quad O$$

Mark went upstairs to get changed. He'd finished his glass of wine downstairs and was trying to decide whether or not to go out to the pub. He didn't go out very often anymore, but he wasn't sure he wanted to stay in tonight. Not now anyway.

He reached his hand out to open the bedroom door, but just before he touched the handle he stopped. He'd heard something, or at least sensed it, and he knew Fiona was in there. He wasn't ready for another row.

For a moment he just stood there, arm outstretched, unsure of what to do next. He sighed and his arm fell to his side, but he didn't move. It was almost as if his brain couldn't process what was going on. Then there was a noise in the bedroom and it shook him from his inactivity. He turned smartly and walked across the hall to his office.

The stairs in the house started near the front door and came out in the centre of the landing. At the top of the stairs, William's parents' room was on the right. William's dad had an office, which was on the left, while his mum's office was directly opposite the stairs. Both offices had a small desk and a bookshelf with different folders and books on them, but they also had a sofa bed and a small wardrobe and were used as guest rooms if anyone came to stay.

If you were still standing at the top of the stairs, then William's room was to the left and slightly behind. His room had a window which looked out to the front of the house and William often spent time gazing out at the village and wondering what his friends were doing. He'd been doing this a lot recently as it was a good way to try and ignore the 'whispers' coming from his parents when they were having another one of their fights. On the walls of his room were a mixture of Star Wars posters and stickers of teddy bears from old birthday cards.

Mark marched past William's room and into his office. He'd decided he was going to check what meetings he had on Monday and then maybe spend some time preparing for them. He just wanted to be active doing something.

His desk was near the window which looked out onto the back garden, and he leaned across to switch his computer on before he sat down. As he pulled the chair out he saw a movement out of the corner of his eye in the garden. He glanced again and saw William running up and down.

He felt a bit guilty as he hadn't even realised William was still outside. He glanced at this watch and then got annoyed at Fiona for letting William be out so late. He'd switch his computer on, he thought, then go and tell her that it just wasn't good enough.

But as he glanced down at William running, something about it caught his attention. It was the speed, or intensity, or maybe it was the fact he seemed to be chatting with friends. Whatever it was, Mark couldn't take his eyes off his son in the back garden.

After the press ups, they were told they had to repeat the sprints and do the same exercises again. This time Billy ran even harder and faster and his team managed to win. All the losers had to do twenty star jumps this time and it was Billy's team's turn to jeer and laugh at them.

○   ○   ○

Fiona stood at the bedroom window, staring at William, unable to tear her eyes away. She was watching with a sense of pride at the effort and passion William was showing, but she also felt a sense of loneliness wash over her. This was exactly what she wanted to be sharing with Mark. Watching their little boy almost grow up before their eyes was what parents should do together - and he did look so grown up down there.

Fiona thought she still loved Mark; but she only thought it, she no longer truly felt it. She thought more about how sad she was, and how sad it was they weren't watching this together, yet she also felt that she wouldn't have enjoyed it as much if he was there.

She didn't know what had happened to them, but she knew something had.

○   ○   ○

Once the running was over, everyone had to do some strength exercises. It started with press-ups and sit-ups, then they had to do squats, keeping their feet on the ground and sitting down until they almost sat on their heels to then standing back up straight again. After the squats they all had to do a plank, resting their weight just on their forearms and toes and keeping their body as flat as possible, they had to hold this position for a minute. It was horrible!

The coaches thought it was funny to throw some rugby balls at the players as they stayed in the plank position. Billy got hit on the bum by one, which nearly made him lose his balance.

They repeated all those exercises again and then again. By the fourth time Billy's plank was really hurting his stomach muscles and a few of the other players had to stop well before the minute was over.

After four rounds of exercises the coaches gave them another drink break.

$$O \quad O \quad O$$

Mark could see William taking a break and having a drink from his water bottle. It was his old one with a cartoon character on it and Mark realised he'd have to buy William a new one.

He loved doing that. Just buying those little things for William. He knew that he'd always do this for his boy, no matter what happened.

William had finished his little drink break and had started again, but Mark couldn't work out what he was doing, as he didn't seem to be anywhere near the rugby ball. In fact, he seemed to be just walking around. Yet even without the ball, and at such a slow pace, Mark could still tell, somehow, William was playing rugby.

After the drink break the team was split up into forwards and backs and they did some tactical work. The coaches put them into their positions on the pitch and without a ball, walked them through where they should be when they needed to defend different positions and scenarios in a real match. Billy was told the times he needed to make sure he was in a flat line, or when he should drop deeper to support the full back.

Once they had walked through every scenario a couple of times each, the coaches added a rugby ball to the session, but they still only jogged, concentrating more on being in the right place and getting the patterns right.

At one stage, Billy made a mistake and joined the line when he should have dropped deep and his coach yelled at him. He was made to do ten press-ups before he could join in again and everyone ran through the same move a couple of extra times just so Billy could get it right and remember it.

Then they were told they were going to practise two new attacking moves to help them to beat the opposition and score a try. The first involved the scrum half kicking the ball to the winger, so Billy and the rest of the backs just had to make sure they were in the right position as they walked it through. The second though, was a move designed for Billy to sprint through and attack the opposition.

The coaches called it 'running a new line' and Billy had to start a bit deeper than normal and instead of talking his normal position in the line as outside centre he was to run at a different angle and receive the ball at inside centre and then run diagonally towards the opposite wing. Once they'd walked it through and everyone seemed to understand it, they tried it at full speed. The first time someone got in Billy's way as he was running. The second time Billy dropped the ball. But the third time they got it right. They ran through it three more times and each time Billy felt good receiving the ball and sprinting forward.

William was walking around the garden nodding to himself and looking around as if to check where he was.

It was very strange to watch and Fiona nearly called out to Mark to see if he was watching it too, but at the last moment she stopped herself. If he wasn't watching, could she really explain what she was seeing? And besides, although she knew it was selfish, she somehow wanted to keep this for herself.

And then the walking stopped and all she could see was an intensity of action in the garden below her. William was still there on his own, but somehow the garden suddenly became a blur of activity.

O   O   O

The coaches then brought the forwards in to join the backs. Although they were all out of position, they were going to act as the opposition so the backs could practise those attacking moves with real people in front of them.

For the first move, the scrum half got it completely wrong, twice, and kicked the ball too far; straight into one of the forwards' hands, giving the winger no chance at all to chase after it. On the third attempt they got it right, but by now the forwards knew what to expect. So as the winger caught the ball, he ran straight into two forwards who tackled him, laughing, to the ground.

The backs then prepared for Billy's move. This time they got it perfect the first time. Although he was only running against slightly slower forwards, Billy burst through the line, completely wrong footing them and ran to the try line. A few metres out, the full back got ready to tackle him, but Billy had the time and confidence to do a dummy pass and then run round the full back to gleefully score his try.

O   O   O

Mark laughed to himself. It was a perfect dummy pass and William was now celebrating the 'try' he had scored.

So that's what he was practising, he thought to himself, and he watched as William celebrated and although the garden was empty, he seemed to be hugged and high-fived by teammates.

Suddenly Mark realised the time and opened his office window.

"Great dummy pass!" he shouted down to William. "But it's time to come in now."

○ ○ ○

Fiona had opened the window just after Mark and was about to call William in herself. So, he was watching, she thought to herself and then she smiled as William first put his thumb up to reply to his dad, but then when he saw her from the other window, put his thumb up to her too.

○ ○ ○

"Great work, everyone," said the coach. "If we can do that in a match there's every chance we'll score some extra tries."

Billy grinned and put his thumb up to the coach.

"Great work, Billy!" said the team captain, who was one of the forwards Billy had skipped past to score his try, and Billy put his other thumb up to him as well.

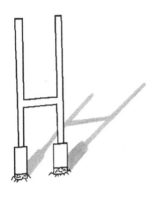

10

There was a strange atmosphere at the breakfast table the next morning, but William didn't notice. All he could think about was rugby and scoring tries. It was as if he'd had the most amazing dream and if he closed his eyes and thought carefully, he could remember it almost as if it had actually happened. He even felt sore and bruised as though all those tackles had been real.

Next to him at the table though, his parents were even quieter than usual. If William hadn't been so caught up in his rugby thoughts, he'd have realised no-one was talking and it was almost as if his parents were also trying to eat even more quietly.

The strange mood continued over the weekend and eventually William did start to notice. By Monday morning, he was actually keen to go to school. He was still excited by the rugby training, but he was also glad to be able to leave his parents, with their sighs and silences, behind

After breakfast on Monday morning, William jumped up from the table,

"Bye, Mum, bye, Dad, I'm off to school."

"Wait for me, William. You know you can't walk on your own yet," his mum called after him.

"Ok," William groaned. "But hurry up, cos I want to get there early."

"Wow, what's the rush?" his mum asked as she put her shoes on. But William just shrugged. As she stepped out of the door she turned back and looked at William's dad, who in all the rush around him was still finishing his toast, "We'll definitely talk at lunchtime, then?" she asked. He nodded.

"Right then, you. What's got you so excited for school?"

"There's another rugby match soon and the team will be announced today," said William, as he walked so quickly down the road his mum almost had to run to keep up with him.

William had one of his best mornings ever at school. In Maths, they were doing long division and for the past three lessons William had really struggled with it. Whenever Miss Heath had explained it again to him he understood, but when she moved away to help someone else and he had to work out the next example on his own, it felt as though all the knowledge had been poured out of his head.

Today though, things were different. Today, William didn't even need to ask Miss Heath to help. Someone had put a cork in the bottle and all the knowledge was staying in his head and he could answer all the questions.

After Maths, they had English and Miss Heath wanted the class to read from the text. William normally hated this. He could feel his face getting redder and redder when it was his turn to read and then he would stumble over the words, which of course made him go redder. Sometimes, it felt as if it wasn't until halfway through break his face returned to a normal colour. But today, William surprised himself, all of his classmates, and Miss Heath, by volunteering to go first.

At break he met up with Tom and Finlay as normal. But just as he was walking over to them, Stephen and Harry saw him and sauntered over.

"Drop anything else lately?" said Harry.

William dropped his head and looked at his shoes. He looked as if he would cry at any moment and he mumbled his reply.

"What!?" demanded Harry.

William didn't lift his head and just mumbled again.

"What!? Speak up, dropper!"

William lifted his head and a big grin spread across his face,

"I said, 'Idiots say what'" and he laughed as he ran towards Tom and Finlay. Even Stephen had started to laugh until Harry punched him.

"Rubbish at rugby!" Harry shouted after him. But William carried on laughing.

"I know you are, but what about me?" he called out.

By this time, Tom and Finlay were laughing too and the three of them walked off together. Harry just punched Stephen again.

William knew the rugby team for the next match was due to be posted at the end of the school day and slowly, as the day passed, nerves started to affect his happy mood.

The last lesson of the day was Science and the class was able to use the science equipment. William could barely sit still, but fortunately, they had to do an experiment during the second half of the lesson so William could stand up at the desk.

They had to test liquids to see how thick they were. They had water, syrup, oil and some others to run down a surface and time. However, William's nerves were getting so bad he spilled the fairy liquid all over the desk - twice!

As soon as the bell went for the end of the lesson, William packed his bag and stood by the door ready to leave.

"Okay, everyone, off you...." But William didn't hear the rest of what Miss Heath said as he was already rushing out of the door and heading towards the notice board where the rugby team was posted.

As he arrived at the notice board, William suddenly felt even more nervous. He really wanted to play again, and even more so now he felt like he was somehow getting extra practice in as Billy.

"Hey, William! See you at the match." It was Alex again and he was walking away from the teamsheet with a grin on his face and his thumbs up to William.

William's knees almost buckled with relief, but he needed to see for himself. He didn't care about nudging into any of the Year 6 boys and even pushed past Stephen to get to the board - and there was his name next to the Number 13 on the teamsheet. He'd been picked!

By the time Tom and Finlay caught up with him, William was walking away from the noticeboard with an enormous grin on his face.

"Been picked then?" asked Tom.

"Might have been," replied William.

"That's a pretty big smile for someone who only 'might' have been picked," said Finlay and they all laughed.

William felt like skipping home and as the three of them crossed the park he ran forward laughing. He soon realised neither Tom nor Finlay were running with him, so he ran back to them, came up behind them and gave them both a gentle kick up the bum.

"Come on, you two, let's go."

"Alright, rugby boy!" said Tom, trying to be angry, but not quite managing it. "The two of us are actually just being normal, you're the one being weird." But Tom couldn't resist and suddenly sprinted across the field and sat on one of the swings. William joined him and they had both managed to swing themselves quite high by the time Finlay caught up with them.

"It seems to be a competition as to who is the craziest," said Finlay laughing at them both. So as if to prove he was the craziest, Tom leapt off the swing when it was in mid-air and rolled on the ground, before jumping up with a big grin.

William slowed his swing down and got off and then he and Finlay went on the see-saw for a few minutes.

"Your mum's waving at you," said Tom and William looked up and could see his mum in the corner of the field, where she normally met him, waving her arms. But she wasn't waving, instead she was beckoning William over.

The three of them hurried over to the corner of the park. William was still very excited,

"Hey, guess what, Mum?"

"Not now, William," his mum replied. "I've brought the car. In you get. Come on, quickly!"

110

William's mum never normally picked William up in the car, not even on the days when it was raining and William secretly hoped she had brought it.

"Bye, Tom, bye, Finlay," he said as he followed his mum to where she was parked.

"So, you'll never guess what," William said as he got into his seat.

"Not now, please," his mum said. "Let's just get home." So, William sat in silence while they drove home.

When they got home his dad was already home, which was unusual, but William was just excited to be able to tell him his news.

"Hey, Dad, you're home," William said as he burst through the door. "The best thing ever happened today..."

But his dad cut him off before he could get any further,

"Not right now, Champ. Why don't you just sit down in the kitchen for a minute?"

William sat at the kitchen table with his dad, still excited about his news, and his mum joined the two of them. William's mum and dad looked at each other and gave each other a strange smile. Nobody spoke for a few seconds and William was just about to launch into his news when both of his parents cleared their throats.

Then a few more seconds of silence. William couldn't work out what this was all about.

All of a sudden, they both spoke at once,

"William..." Then they both gave a nervous laugh. William's mum looked at his dad and his dad just shrugged.

"William, your dad and I have something to tell you," she started.

William looked at them both, but his dad was staring at the table.

"The thing is... well, what we want to say... what both of us want to say," and William's dad looked up and nodded and smiled at William. "What both of us want to say is that we love you very much."

William's mum took a deep breath and carried on.

"But the thing is, Mummy and Daddy don't love each other as much as we should at the moment."

William was starting to feel worried. This was a very strange conversation and on top of that, they never called themselves 'Mummy' and 'Daddy' anymore. William wasn't a baby!

"We still love you, Champ," his dad said, "and having you as a son makes me, well, both of us, so happy. But the thing is, these days, we don't make each other very happy. You've probably noticed that over the last few weeks."

William had noticed that they weren't very happy, but he just thought this was how adults were.

"So," it was his mum's turn now. "So, the thing is, we've decided to try and do something about it and spend some time apart for a while."

"What do you mean, 'time apart'?" asked William. "We all live together in this house. How can you be apart?"

"Well, that's exactly it," said his dad. "We think it's best if mum moves out of this house for a little while and you and I stay here."

"What? ... But... I mean, you live here... Where can you go? Why are you going?" William couldn't quite grasp what was going on. He understood all the words his parents had said, but he didn't understand why they were saying them. He started to cry and he didn't know why. He wanted to be a baby again. He wanted them to be his mummy and daddy like they used to be. He wanted this conversation to stop.

His mum had brought her chair closer to William's and she held him as he cried.

"I will always really, really love you ... and I won't be far away ... and I'll still see you lots and lots."

But William didn't want to hear any of this and he shrugged her off and ran out of the kitchen.

"I don't want you to go," he sobbed as he ran up the stairs to his bedroom. He slammed the door and then cried on his bed.

After a few minutes, he stopped crying and just lay on his bed. He still wasn't sure he knew what it all meant, but he did know he didn't like it.

There was a knock at the door and his dad peered round the door.

"Can I come in, Champ?" he asked. William nodded and his dad came in and sat on his bed.

"We meant it when we said we will never stop loving you, you know," he said. "It's the best thing in the world being your dad and I know your mum thinks the same, well, you know, about being your mum, not your dad, obviously." And in spite of everything, William couldn't help but smile.

"The thing is, I love being your dad, but I'm sometimes not a very good husband to your mum. I get stuff wrong and sometimes make your mum unhappy, so she wants some time away for a bit. She's not leaving you, she loves you. But she needs some time away from me for a while."

His dad explained to William that his mum had a friend who had a flat above a shop in the village and so she was going to live there for a while. She would see William every week and even walk him to school once a week. But part of all the changes meant that she would be able to work more, which apparently was what she wanted and needed to do right now. At the same time, William's dad was going to work less, because he said this was one of the reasons that his mum was unhappy. So, William's dad was going to work from home and be there to look after William more.

William's mum would be able to stay in the flat until January, so they weren't going to make any other changes, but just see how this worked for now. It meant Christmas would be a bit different this year, but William's dad kept saying it would be 'absolutely fine' and they'd 'work it out' and he loved William to the moon and back.

"I know you wouldn't have chosen any of this, and you probably don't really understand it all," his dad said to William. "And I know I've said this loads already, but we love you, both of us. And it really will be ok. But Mummy and Daddy need to do this."

"Now, I'd like you to do me a big favour." William sat up and nodded ok. "I'd like you to go downstairs and give your mum a big hug. She's really upset that you're upset and she wants to give you a cuddle. Will you do that for me?"

William nodded again, wiped his face with the back of his hand and went downstairs to find his mum. She was sitting in exactly the same place at the kitchen table, but now there was a glass of wine in front of her. It was her turn to wipe the tears from her eyes as William entered the kitchen.

"Hello, sweetheart. Are you ok?" she whispered and held out her arms for him.

William couldn't find any words to say. He wasn't even sure whether he should nod his head. So instead, he almost fell into her arms and they cuddled and cried together.

Despite all of the tears, from all three of them, they still sat down to dinner together. It was pasta with a tomato sauce and William found he was starvingly hungry.

Later that night as William was getting ready for bed, his dad came into his bedroom.

"Hey, sorry, Champ, didn't you want to tell us something earlier? What was it, do you want to tell me now?"

"It doesn't matter," William said, "it's nothing."

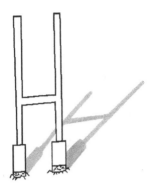

11

That weekend was a very strange one. William's mum and dad suggested he spend the Saturday round at Finlay's house - his mum had already phoned Finlay's mum to ask her if it was ok before they had spoken to William about it. So, straight after breakfast, William had been driven round to see Finlay.

Finlay was pleased to see him and was excited to teach William a couple of different card games that he normally played with his mum. For lunch, they ate sandwiches in front of the television and Finlay's mum had even bought a cake, which, just for once, they were allowed to eat in front of the television, too.

After lunch, they sat and watched cartoons and it made William feel safe. Even when some of the more babyish cartoons came on, they continued to watch.

Part of William wanted to return to how his life had been a few years before, when he had watched those cartoons almost non-stop.

However, all the time he was watching TV, William's mind couldn't help thinking about what was happening at home. He wanted to know what was so terrible that he had to be here, and not at home with his mum and dad. In the end, he couldn't sit still any longer - watching the cartoons with half of his brain, while the other half was thinking about home. He jumped off the sofa and almost shouted at Finlay,

"Can we play rugby?"

Finlay, startled by William's sudden movement and question stuttered,

"Erm... well... n-n-not really. I don't have a rugby ball."

Suddenly, it was all too much for William and he sat back down as quickly as he had stood up. The cushion on the sofa let out some air and it sounded like a fart and William knew that he would have laughed on almost any other day, but today he just screwed his eyes up and tried not to cry.

He sat like that for several seconds. He'd turned his back on Finlay and squeezed his eyes as tight as he could. Two tears escaped and slowly dripped down his cheeks, but considering how upset he was feeling William was surprised there weren't more. Finally, he opened his eyes, wiped them with the back of his sleeve and turned back round to face Finlay. But all he saw was an empty seat.

William couldn't help himself, even he hates me now, he thought. This time floods of tears escaped and he didn't try to stop them.

After what seemed like minutes and minutes of crying, but was probably only a few seconds, William realised Finlay had come back into the room. William jumped up and wiped away his tears. He started to try and make up an excuse about the cartoons being sad, but Finlay just ignored him. In fact, he acted as if he hadn't even seen William crying at all.

"Sorry for disappearing," said Finlay. "But my mum asked me if she could take us both to the swimming pool. Apparently, there's a session this afternoon with the water slides. Do you fancy it?"

Now it was William's turn to almost stutter.

"Well, I mean... we could, I mean... what about trunks?"

"Don't worry about that, I've got a couple of pairs of swimming shorts and I'm sure one of them will fit you. So, shall I tell my mum we want to go?"

William just nodded. Finlay grinned and ran out of the room again shouting to his mum.

Almost immediately, Finlay's mum appeared with a bag packed with swimming kit and towels.

"Thanks for letting me take you," she said to William. "Finlay's wanted to go and try it out for ages, but I don't swim, so I didn't want him to go on his own. Right then, let's go."

She bundled the boys and the bag full of swimming kit into the car and they were off. As they pulled out of Finlay's road, Finlay's mum turned round to the boys in the back seat and held out her hand. In it were two individually wrapped chocolate biscuits.

"Thanks, Mum," said Finlay grinning. He took the biscuits, passed one to William and turned to him and asked, "So, who is your favourite Transformer?"

William answered through a mouthful of biscuit and, of course, Finlay disagreed with him and told him why his choice of Transformer was much better, but it was all done in a friendly way. Before long William couldn't remember why he had been crying and instead was laughing at Finlay's impression of trying to change himself into a robot.

It didn't take long to get to the swimming pool. Finlay's mum paid for them to go in and told them they had just over an hour to go, and enjoy all the slides.

"Make sure you stay together and get out when the whistle is blown," she said. "I'll be in the café when you're done."

120

"Ok!" They ran off to the changing rooms. The next hour was full of swimming, splashing and sliding - they had the best time - ever!

$$\circ \quad \circ \quad \circ$$

Once they were both dry and dressed, they met up with Finlay's mum in the café. She had two hot chocolates and two more chocolate biscuits waiting for them.

"Was that fun?" The boys could only nod their heads as their mouths were full of biscuits and hot chocolate. But they nodded their heads a lot. Finlay's mum laughed,

"Ok, I'll take that as a yes then."

They walked out of the leisure centre and into the dark evening. It took them a few minutes to find the car as everything looked so different in the dark, but they were soon in it and driving off.

"William, I'd like to ask you to stay for tea, but I'm afraid I don't really have anything in I could feed you both," said Finlay's mum.

"No, that's..." William was about to say it was fine, but he didn't have chance to finish his sentence before Finlay's mum spoke again.

"So, I thought I'd take you both to McDonald's if that's ok."

"Yay!" Both boys cheered in the back of the car and then started to discuss which slide had been the best, who had been the fastest to slide down and who had made the biggest splash in the pool at the end.

After a meal of cheeseburgers, chips, some nuggets to share and a milkshake each, William had strawberry and Finlay had chocolate, they were back in the car driving home.

"Ok, William, I'm going to drop you off at home now, but you can always come round again anytime you like. You know, if things ever get... erm... awkward for you at home," said Finlay's mum as she drove.

William suddenly remembered what was waiting for him back home and just nodded. He sat quietly for the rest of the journey and not even Finlay's questions about rugby could elicit more than a nod or a grunt from him.

"Right then, here we are," said Finlay's mum as she pulled onto the drive, in front of William's house.

"Thank you for a lovely afternoon, Mrs... Finlay's Mum," said William. Finlay's mum laughed,

"Call me Sharon. You're very welcome and remember what I said, you're invited round any time."

"Yeah, thanks," said William, but he still didn't call her 'Sharon'.

He turned to Finlay and wanted to hug him, but he wasn't sure if he should. Instead, he started to give him a high five, but because he had leant forward slightly as if to hug him, the high five looked more like he was about to punch Finlay.

"Oh no, sorry! I didn't mean that. I was just gonna, but that I, well you know, I... anyway, I just wanted to say thanks."

"You've got a funny way of saying thanks," Finlay laughed and put up his fists like a boxer. He put them down again as he said, "Thanks for coming round. Without you my mum would never have taken me swimming, or to McDonalds. Please come round again." Then he raised his hand so they could properly high five each other.

William jumped out of the car and he could hear Finlay's mum tell Finlay to sit still for a minute. William knocked on the front door and it was opened almost straight away by his mum.

"Oh, hello, you. A good day?" his mum asked. "Oh, Sharon, thanks so much for this afternoon..."

As William walked through the door, he saw one of the pictures in the hallway had been taken off the wall. Then he saw the door to the cupboard where all the shoes were stored was open, he looked inside and realised half the shoes were missing. That was strange. He looked again and it wasn't that half the shoes were missing, but *all* his mum's shoes.

William ran around the house looking for anything else missing or out of place. He opened doors and looked into the room then closed it and went to the next door. Again and again he did this, opening some doors three or four times. He went upstairs and checked the bathroom, his room and his parents' room.

When his mum closed the front door she found him staring into the kitchen.

"Hey there, what are you doing?"

"I'm just checking."

"Checking what?" she asked

"Checking to see what you're taking," he said pushing past her and going to have another look in the front room. This time he went into the room and started to carefully look at all the shelves and the books, CDs, DVDs and ornaments.

"Wasn't there an elephant or something here?" he said, pointing to one of the shelves.

"It was a tiger, yes," his mum replied. "It was something Granny and Pops got for me when I was a little girl."

But William wasn't really listening. Instead, he just turned and pointed to another shelf,

"And there was a clock here."

"That was an old clock which I inherited from my grandparents."

"And some of the books are missing," William said, becoming almost hysterical now.

"I'm going to need something to read," his mum said.

"WELL, YOU CAN'T TAKE THEM! YOU CAN'T TAKE ANY OF THEM!" William ran upstairs and slammed his bedroom door behind him as he fell onto his bed and started to cry.

A few minutes later his mum knocked on the door.

"Go awaaaaay!" William said, his voice trembling, but the door opened anyway.

William's mum sat down on his bed and gently laid her hand on his back. She didn't speak. After a couple of minutes, she shuffled her bottom to give William the hint he needed to move across his bed to give her more room. She still didn't speak. William didn't look up and just hugged his pillow, but he had stopped crying. His mum shuffled her bottom again and William moved up against his wall and his mum lay down next to him. Without looking at her, William let go of his pillow and hugged his mum instead.

"I don't want you to go," he said eventually.

"I know."

"I want you to stay and for things to be like normal."

"I know."

"I don't understand what went wrong, was it something I did?"

"No! Definitely not!" said William's mum. "Please never think that. I know it's hard for you, but it is not your fault. And I definitely don't want to leave you," she said.

"Then stay," pleaded William.

"It's not that simple," sighed his mum. "I want to stay, but... but I can't. Your dad and I aren't happy right now - nothing to do with you, we both love you - but we're not sure if we love each other anymore. It gets complicated when you're an adult. I've got a really good chance to do well at work, maybe a promotion, so it means I'll need to work some long hours."

William just shrugged and lay back down on the bed hugging his pillow. His mum stroked his back.

"I love you. I will always love you. And I won't be far away, just in the flat over McGill's shop, you know the funny antique one. I'll see you every week."

She carried on rubbing his back, but William didn't respond. Eventually his breathing got softer and he fell asleep, still in his clothes and still angry at his mum, but not so angry it kept him awake.

$$O \quad O \quad O$$

The following morning the atmosphere around the breakfast table was very strained. William wasn't in the mood to talk, but he could tell his parents were trying hard to talk to each other and to be 'normal'. It was weird. They didn't talk to each other this much when they had actually been getting on. But now they were talking about everything. And being so polite. There were so many 'pleases', 'thank yous' and 'you're welcomes' William felt like he was in an American TV show.

After he'd finished his Cheerios, William made his excuses, left the table, and went upstairs to his bedroom. He wanted to leave them to it - whatever it was - as much as possible.

William lay on his bed and read for most of the morning. He had actually finished his reading book, but he was so determined not to go downstairs again that he read one of his school science books for an hour. While he was reading, he could hear things moving and being put down again, drawers rattling, doors opening and closing and still lots of 'pleases', 'thank yous' and 'you're welcomes'. At one stage William had put his pillow over his head just to escape it all.

About half an hour later, there was a knock at William's door and his dad's head appeared.

"Right then, Champ. Get your shoes, you and I are going for a walk."

"Eh? We never go for a walk."

"Well, we are now."

"I don't want to go for a...," but William was cut off by his dad.

"It wasn't a question. I wasn't asking your permission. I was telling you. Now, off the bed, downstairs, shoes on, let's go," his dad said.

Although his dad was still smiling and trying to look cheerful, there was something in the tone of his voice which made William not want to question him again. He jumped off his bed and went downstairs to put his shoes on.

William's dad had got their coats, scarves and gloves ready while William was putting his shoes on, and it was a good job he had, as it was freezing cold outside. It was bright and sunny, but the sun didn't seem to have enough power to actually warm the day up. However, once they got moving William felt less chilly and nice and toasty in his coat and scarf.

They walked along their road until they came to the end. William had assumed that his dad had just gone the wrong way until he saw a gap in the hedge and a little path going down the hill on the other side of the hedge.

"I didn't even know this was here," he said to his dad.

"That's because you never go out for a walk," his dad replied. "Although to be honest, we've lived here about four months now and I think this is only the second time I've ever been this way."

William smiled at his dad and they carried on walking. A few metres in front of them was a road, which William thought he recognised, but he was already confused. They crossed the road and there was another path they followed for about five minutes.

As the path came to another road they crossed it and walked up a slight hill. The road was the kind that if you were in a car you would call 'twisty and turny'. They weren't walking fast enough to feel the same sensation, but every hundred metres or so they would turn a corner. Most of the first few minutes along this road had been up a gentle slope with big hedges on either side which had fields behind them. Some had sheep or horses in them, some were ploughed, while others had wild grass growing.

"Are we still in Northbrook?" William asked at one point.

"Of course we are, we've not walked that far," his dad chuckled. "It does look a bit different out here though, doesn't it? I suppose we're on the edge of the town. Wait a few minutes and you'll see what I mean."

They walked for a few more minutes, as the road got a bit steeper, until they reached the top and it flattened out and turned away to their left. Just after the turn there was a large area where the hedge was missing and suddenly William could see down onto Northbrook.

"Oh wow! Is that Northbrook?"

"That's right. Where else did you think it might be?"

"No, I know," said William. "It's just I've never seen it from up here before. It's, well, it's big, isn't it?" His dad laughed and nodded.

"I suppose it is quite big really. But I bet we can work out where a few places you know are. Look, there's your school."

They spent a few minutes looking down onto the town trying to spot some of the places William knew in the town. They could see William's school and from there they could work out where Finlay's house was; they could see the road Tom lived on, but they didn't think they could see his actual house. They couldn't see round to their road, but they could see the road which led to it.

They set off again and the road started to go back downhill. Soon they were walking past William's school which they had seen from above a few moments earlier. They turned and walked through the centre of the town and then stopped at a red door which William was fairly sure he had never seen before. It was squashed in between two shops and had an ornate door handle.

There was a buzzer just to the side of the door and William's dad pressed it. A response crackled through it which William couldn't hear properly.

"Hi, it's us," he said and the door clicked and his dad pushed it open.

"I don't understand," said William, "what are we doing?"

"Just go on up, you'll see," his dad replied.

William went in first. Immediately in front of the door was a set of stairs. At the top of the stairs was a small landing with a door off to either side. The door on the left was open and standing in the doorway was his mum.

"Hey!" his mum said, with her arms open wide to give him a hug. "Come and see my new flat."

William looked back to his dad, but he just waved him forward, so in he went.

William stepped in and his mum wrapped him in her arms and started to walk down the short hallway with him.

"I'll just wait h...," his dad started to say when his mum cut him off.

"Don't be silly, Mark, you're invited in as well. Of course you are." So, they both went into the new flat, where his mum would now be living.

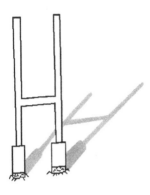

12

It was on Monday morning, when he got up to get ready for school, that William truly realised things were different. It started with his dad waking him up 15 minutes later than his mum normally did. Then, his dad didn't know where his lunchbox was stored and finally, for at least five minutes, neither of them could find his school shoes - until they realised they had actually been put away in the cupboard.

By the time they set off to walk to school they were both feeling a bit stressed and they were running late.

"Come on, hurry up!" said William's dad as they marched through the village. William's dad was striding ahead and William almost had to run to keep up with him. As they entered the churchyard he looked at his watch again and yelled at William, "HURRY UP!"

When they arrived at the other side of the churchyard they saw Tom and Finlay standing together.

"Hurry up, slow coach," called Tom, "we'll be late if we're not careful." Tom grabbed William and dragged him along to where Finlay was standing, waiting impatiently.

"Bye, Mrs... oh sorry, Mr Brown," he yelled over his shoulder as the three of them walked across the field to school.

"See you after school, William," his dad called after them, but William was already out of earshot.

"How come your dad walked with you this morning?" asked Tom.

"Well, you know, he just did," William mumbled in reply. Finlay looked at him smiled and then changed the subject to talk about a film he had watched over the weekend. Tom hadn't seen it, but it didn't stop him calling the movie 'stupid'. By the time they had arrived at school, Tom had forgotten his question about William's dad.

William was quiet for most of the day at school. Tom had asked him if he was ok a couple of times, but William just shrugged him off. It didn't seem to matter to Tom as he was in one of his extra talkative days and he talked enough for the both of them. In fact, Tom got told off three times by Miss Heath for talking in class.

At the end of the day as the boys were walking over the field, Tom tried to ask why his was dad picking him up from school. Instead of being quiet, William snapped,

"He just is! Ok?" he yelled at Tom and ran off ahead of

the other two. Tom looked bemused and tried to chase after William, but Finlay stopped him.

"Leave him," Finlay said. "I think his dad's going to be walking with him for a few days, so I'd just drop it if I was you."

"Yeah, but I was only..."

"I know, but best to just drop it," Finlay said. Tom shrugged his shoulders and carried on walking.

Tom and Finlay walked together up to Finlay's house, then Tom walked on to his own house. As he walked, he had to pass William who was standing where he usually met his mum after school. Of course, today she wasn't there - and neither was his dad.

"See ya, William," Tom yelled as he walked past. William just mumbled his reply.

"Look," said Tom, "I didn't mean to upset you." But William turned so his back was facing Tom and looked down at the floor.

"Oh, forget it then. Suit yourself," and Tom carried on walking while William waited. And waited.

William realised it was starting to get dark and he wondered what he should do. Should he try and walk home on his own? Maybe, but it was quite a long way and he was pretty sure his dad would be angry with him if he did. Maybe he could walk to his mum's new flat. It was closer, but what if she wasn't in? Finlay's house was only just round the corner and he knew Finlay's mum was nice. Ok, he would walk to Finlay's he decided. He would just give it one more minute.

Just as he was about to set off to Finlay's he heard panting behind him.

"William! William!" It was his dad calling. "William, I'm so sorry I'm late. It's just I was working ... and then I realised the time ... and so I came as quickly as I could ... it's just ..."

His dad was still panting as he spoke, so it was hard for William to hear him. Part of William was relieved he had turned up. Part of him even felt a little bit sorry for his dad. But mostly William was angry and he didn't want to listen to any more excuses.

"Mum was never late to meet me," he said as he stormed off towards home. He knew this wasn't entirely true as he could remember at least two times she was late, but he didn't care right now.

"William, wait!" his dad called as he jogged after him.

William decided he was going to sulk about this for the whole evening, in the end he even took himself to bed before his dad told him it was time.

The next day at school William was still in a bad mood, but this time Tom didn't ask him any questions about it, which was probably a good idea. But because he couldn't snap at Tom, William found the anger just grew and grew inside him all day. He sat with Tom and Finlay at lunch time, but he barely said a word to them. He just stared across the playground.

When one of the girls caught her foot in a skipping rope and fell over, William just laughed. She had cut her knee and it was bleeding quite badly. Her friends called for the teacher while she sat on the floor crying. William laughed again.

"That's not very kind," said Finlay. "She might be really hurt."

"It was funny," was William's only reply and he turned away from Finlay and continued staring across the playground. A few minutes later when the bell went, William, still staring across the playground, slowly got up to walk back into the school building. He was ten paces into the walk before he realised Tom and Finlay weren't next to him and were already walking through the door into school.

The queues going up the stairs and into the classrooms meant William had caught up with Tom by the time they walked through the door into their classroom in time for Geography. But instead of speaking to Tom, William barged past him, banging his shoulder into Tom and making Tom stumble into a desk.

"Oi! What was that for?"

"Yeah well, I wouldn't have done it to a friend," said William.

"What do you mean? Of course I'm your friend," Tom replied.

"Well why did you walk off? You two left me."

"You were just staring, mate. We tried to say something, but you were like a robot." Tom started to move his arms and legs stiffly and walk like an old-fashioned robot. "I. Am. William."

"No, I wasn't. Stop it!" said William and pushed Tom towards his desk.

"Right, everyone. Settle down and books out," said Miss Heath from the front of the class. "Did you all just have sweets for lunch? Come on, settle down now."

The rest of the class started to quieten down, but Tom had heard a few people giggle at his robot impression, so carried on, although more quietly now.

"I. Am. William. I. Am. William." More people laughed, so Tom got even louder, "I. Am. William."

Miss Heath looked up from her desk and stood up to calm everyone down again, but just as she did William stood up and stomped round to the front of Tom's desk.

"I SAID STOP IT!" he yelled. Then he pushed all of Tom's books and pens off his desk onto the floor.

"OUT! NOW!" Miss Heath pointed to the door and William went outside and stood in the corridor. He knew what he was meant to do. The school rule was you had to wait a few minutes to calm down, then you had to knock on the classroom door and politely ask to be let back in. Sometimes the teacher just let you back in, but sometimes they gave you a note which you then had to take down to the headmaster's office.

William had never been sent out of the classroom before. He sat down for a minute to think about what might happen next and then he started to cry. He wept hot, salty tears for a couple of minutes, upset about how he had treated Tom, but also still confused about what was happening with his parents. After a while he stopped, wiped his face and got ready to knock and ask if he could go back into the classroom. Just as he was about to knock, Harry came round the corner.

"Oi, William, is that Miss Heath's class?" he said, pointing at the door William was about to knock on. William nodded.

"Wait a minute, what are you doing in the corridor? Have you been naughty?" Harry laughed as if the very thought of it was funny. But William nodded again.

"Oh, wow! You're almost one of us now," and he laughed again. "You look like you've been crying though. Maybe not one of us after all, maybe just a little wimp who cries if a teacher tells him off." This time he laughed right in William's face.

Suddenly, all of William's anger came up again. He was angry at Harry for laughing. He was angry at Tom for his stupid robot impression, and at Finlay for walking off at lunch time. He was angry at his dad for being late yesterday and he was angry at his mum for moving out. All this anger burned in William like it was red hot and right in front of him was Harry's stupid face laughing at him. So, William punched him.

He actually punched him quite hard, Harry fell across the corridor and landed on the floor. The note he was carrying for Miss Heath fell out of his hand and lay next to him. Harry slowly stood up. It took him a minute to realise what had happened, but as he felt his chin he remembered.

William wasn't angry anymore; in fact he was a little bit scared. He was right to be scared as Harry suddenly launched himself at William. Harry wasn't scared. Instead, he was now *very* angry.

He ran at William and rugby tackled him around his waist, William fell against the wall and then down onto the floor with Harry on top of him punching him hard. William managed to dodge his head so most of the punches landed on his shoulders, or missed him altogether, but he realised if he didn't move soon one of Harry's fists was going to hit him hard in the face.

William started to swing his own fists. He wasn't really trying to hit Harry, but he was trying to unbalance him and make it harder for Harry to hit him. However, just as Harry leant back to try to hit William even harder, William's fist caught him in the eye. Harry fell backwards and William was able to roll so Harry fell onto the floor and now William was on top of him.

William's random punch had split the skin above Harry's eye and there was blood already starting to trickle down Harry's face. William raised his fist to punch him again. Harry cowered on the floor and put his hands over his face to protect himself. Just at that moment Miss Heath, who had heard the commotion in the corridor, opened the classroom door.

"WILLIAM! STOP! NOW!" William put his fist down and looked up at Miss Heath. Behind Miss Heath, the kids from the class had left their desks and had come to look at what was going on. William could see their faces peering round the door.

Now it was Harry's turn to roll over and William fell back onto the floor, Harry lent over as if to punch William again, but Miss Heath put her arms out and pulled Harry away.

"And you, Harry. Stop it! Both of you stop! Now, wait there." With that Miss Heath knocked on the next classroom door and walked in. "Mrs Ford, sorry to bother your class, but could I ask you to keep an eye on my class for a few minutes please? I need to take these two to see the headmaster," and she pointed back out into the corridor to William and Harry.

"Of course," said Mrs Ford.

Miss Heath turned to address the rest of her class, many of whom were stood in the open doorway trying to see what was happening. "Back to your desks and stay nice and quiet. Mrs Ford is going to keep an eye on you and I'll be back in a couple of minutes."

She left her classroom door open and pointed at William and Harry, and then pointed to the headmaster's office. Miss Heath walked between William and Harry down the corridor and as they were walking, she reached into her pocket and took out a tissue so Harry could wipe away the blood on his face.

Mr Wilson, the headmaster, didn't seem at all surprised to see Harry, but he was shocked to see William.

"William! Well, I didn't expect to see you here for fighting," he said. "Both of you sit down there," he said pointing to two chairs either side of his desk. "And wait. Quietly." He stepped out of his office to talk to Miss Heath. After a couple of minutes, Miss Heath left and walked back down the corridor to her classroom and the headmaster stepped back into his office.

"Harry, please wait outside for me and I'll deal with you in a few minutes. I'm going to talk to William first."

The headmaster then told William how disappointed he was in him and wanted William to explain why he'd been fighting. William couldn't have explained why it happened, or what had happened, even if he'd wanted to. But while the headmaster was talking to him, he was trying very hard to make sure he didn't cry, so he could hardly speak at all. Instead, he just stared at his shoes, nodded and mumbled in what he hoped were the right places.

After a few minutes, Mr Wilson just sighed and stopped trying to interrogate him.

"If you're not going to tell me anything, then I can't really help you, William. However, I want you to be under

140

no illusion we have a very strict policy here about fighting and we will be phoning your parents and you will be sent home for the rest of the day. I will think about any additional punishment. Now, go and wait outside."

William got up, walked out of the office and slumped down on one of the chairs just outside.

"Harry! In here please," the headmaster called and Harry went in for what William assumed would be the same conversation.

As William sat there he felt a wave of different emotions. One of the first was almost a sense of pride for being able to win a fight against Harry, but then he realised Harry might want revenge, so he felt scared too. He was still a bit annoyed with Tom, but he was also sorry for the way he had behaved. But mostly William felt nervous about what his dad was going to say.

When Harry came out of the headmaster's office, the two of them were left to sit there on the chairs outside. Harry got his mobile phone out and started playing games on it. Every time the headmaster's door opened he quickly put it away. William didn't have a phone, so he just sat there, in silence, staring at the floor. He was worried about what was going to happen to him.

After about 15 minutes, Harry's mum arrived. She walked right up to him and slapped him on the top of the head.

"What have I told you about fighting?" And then she gave him another slap. Before he could even answer the question, she knocked on the headmaster's door and went inside.

Harry was still rubbing his head when she came back out again. She walked straight over to her son and this time he ducked down and covered his head with his arm, but instead of a slap she grabbed him by the elbow and tried to lift him up.

"Come on you, up!" Harry stood up. "Is this the boy you were fighting with? Apologise to him."

Harry stood in front of William and started to mumble something William couldn't hear, but all of a sudden he got another slap on his head. "Apologise properly, Harry!"

"I'm sorry, William," Harry said and put his hand out for William to shake.

"Well, go on then," said Harry's mum and William was worried she might slap him, so he shook Harry's hand.

"Right. That's that. Now, you," she said to Harry, "let's get you home." She turned him round so he was facing the door and pushed him towards it. As they were walking down the corridor William could see another slap land on the top of Harry's head and he couldn't help but chuckle a little.

It was another 15 minutes before William's dad arrived. When he did, he looked at William with big questioning eyes. William didn't know what to say, so he just shrugged. His dad sighed, turned away from William and knocked on the headmaster's door.

William expected he would just be a few minutes like Harry's mum had been, but his dad was inside the headmaster's office for ages. When the door finally opened, his dad and the headmaster came out together.

"Now then, William, I'm sorry about what has been happening at home," Mr Wilson said. "But it is still no excuse for your behaviour today. I don't want this to ever happen again. Your dad has promised me it won't. Can you promise me the same?"

William looked at his dad, then at the headmaster.

"Erm... no, I mean yes. Well, I mean it won't happen again."

"Ok then," said Mr Wilson. "I'm sending you home for the rest of the day, but I expect to see you back here in the morning and with no more fighting. Is that clear?"

"Yes," said William quickly.

"Thank you, Mr Wilson," said his dad and shook the headmaster's hand.

William said nothing at all in the car on the way home and as soon as they got inside he ran straight upstairs to his bedroom. He could hear his dad on the phone.

"Yes, that's right, fighting... no, no it's ok I'll deal with it... well no, it wasn't ideal, I've had to cancel a couple of work calls... he's in his room right now... I don't think that's a good idea... yeah I'll tell him... ok, bye."

A few minutes later, there was a knock on William's door and his dad came in.

"Right then, do you want to tell me what is going on?"

143

"Well, it started because Tom was being an idiot... and then Harry called me a baby... and then... and then," but William couldn't speak any more as he found himself crying.

His dad hugged him and William just cried and cried. After several minutes of crying, he let go of his dad, wiped his eyes and said,

"Sorry, Dad. It won't happen again."

"I still want to talk to you about it more, but right now I've got to answer some emails and apologise for missing some work calls when I had to come and collect you. Stay in your room for a bit and we'll talk later."

"Ok, Dad." And William's dad went back to his desk in his office.

About half an hour later, he got up to make himself a cup of tea and opened William's bedroom door to check on him, but although it was only 2:30 in the afternoon, William was fast asleep on his bed. His dad pulled the duvet over him, quietly closed his bedroom door, and tiptoed down the stairs to put the kettle on.

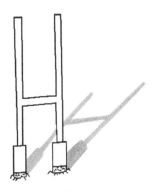

13

"Hey, look, I'm sorry about yesterday," said Tom as soon as he saw William the next morning. "I didn't know about... you know."

Finlay rolled his eyes at Tom's clumsy attempt to apologise, but William didn't seem to mind.

"It's ok," he said. "I'm sorry too. I was just a bit... I don't know... you know... anyway, sorry."

Tom slapped him on his back.

"It's all in the past now," he said. Then he turned round to where William's dad was waiting and watching to see if everything was going to be ok. "Morning, Mr Brown," he yelled. "Don't worry, he's not hit anyone yet." And with that Tom ran off laughing, so William and Finlay chased after him.

One of the conditions of William not being suspended from school was that he had to apologise to Miss Heath and he also had to go and see the headmaster for another 'chat'.

So, as soon as they got to school, instead of hanging around in the playground with Tom and Finlay, William went to the classroom to speak to Miss Heath. He knocked on the door but got no reply, so he cautiously opened the door and stepped inside. At the front of the classroom, Miss Heath was tidying her desk and sorting out some papers, but she had headphones in and was trying to dance as well. As soon as she saw William she pulled the headphones out and William was sure he could see her blush slightly.

"Sorry about that, William. Come on in," she said to him.

William went in and sat at one of the desks at the front of the class.

"We haven't got long before the bell goes, but thank you for coming to see me."

William looked at the floor, but he knew he had to apologise.

"Sorry about yesterday, Miss," he managed.

"William, look at me please." William raised his head and looked at Miss Heath's chin. "Mr Wilson told me what your dad said, so I know this must be an extremely difficult time for you, but don't make things worse by getting yourself into trouble."

William just shrugged his shoulders as he didn't know how to answer that.

Miss Heath carried on. "Don't let yourself get angry about what adults are doing. Especially your parents. Even adults make mistakes. And you're not to blame for what they do, but you can't fix their mistakes either. You just have to carry on doing the best you can do.

But if things are difficult for you, and you ever want to talk to someone, you know you can always talk to me. My parents split up when I was about your age, so I do know what you're going through."

"Really?" said William.

"Yeah, my dad then moved away and I didn't see him at all for nearly four years; it's ok now though and..." And just then the bell went. "OK, go and sit at your desk, but you can chat to me any time," and Miss Heath smiled at William and turned back to sort her papers a bit more before the rest of the class arrived.

William spent the next lesson not able to concentrate, because all he could think about was that a teacher had been through what he was now going through. It didn't seem possible for someone as successful as Miss Heath to have felt like he did now. Of course, he was sad that Miss Heath had ever felt this upset but knowing her story made him feel less alone to deal with his feelings.

At break time, instead of playing with Tom and Finlay in the playground he walked down the corridor to see the headmaster.

As he was waiting outside the headmaster's office, Harry walked in. William tensed up. He was sure not even Harry would try and hit him again right outside the headmaster's office, but he'd probably want to try. After all, you could see the bruise and cut on his face where William had punched him.

But instead, Harry just smiled at William and sat down.

"You've got to have the talking to from the old man as well then have you?" William nodded. "You're actually a pretty good fighter," said Harry. "You know, for a wimp."

William looked up, maybe Harry was trying to wind him up so William would start another fight. But instead, Harry was just smiling.

"If you can fight like that, well, you know, not fight, but tackle and stuff, then you'll be a good rugby player you know."

William was amazed. It was a compliment. From Harry! Before he could answer, the headmaster had called Harry into his office.

After only a couple of minutes, Harry came out again, winked at William and walked off down the corridor. Now it was William's turn to go in.

The chat from the headmaster was all about how he was disappointed in William, how he didn't expect negative behaviour from him and how it was against the ethos of the school. The headmaster told William at least three times if it happened again 'the consequences would be severe.' But after a couple of minutes, he told William that he could go and William left the office as quickly as he could.

He didn't have time to get to the playground, but as they were walking into their Maths lesson immediately after break, Tom came up to him to ask how it had gone. William put his thumb up and they went in to learn about long division.

Over the next few weeks, William slowly adapted to his new way of life. He went to school as normal, but every Wednesday after school he would go to his mum's new flat. He also went every other weekend, and, on those weekends, he would go straight to the flat after school on a Friday and then back to school from his mum's on a Monday morning.

It was a bit strange seeing his mum in her new flat. Some days he'd get confused about where he was meant to be. But he didn't get as confused as his mum one Wednesday, when William buzzed at his mum's door.

"Hello, I'm not expecting a delivery today, but can you just leave it inside the door, please," his mum said as she answered the buzzer and the door clicked open.

William wasn't sure what to do, so he just buzzed again. Before his mum could speak, he shouted into the intercom,

"I'm not a delivery, I'm me."

"Oh my goodness! Oh, I'm so sorry! Is it Wednesday already?"

"Yes!" William replied. "Can you let me up please?"

"Of course, of course. Sorry, sweetheart," his mum said and the door clicked open again.

His mum apologised a lot during the evening and even let William have fish and chips for tea. The following Wednesday when he went round to his mum's again, William buzzed and when she answered he shouted,

"Delivery!"

"Ok, clever clogs," she said and let him upstairs.

His mum was actually very busy with her new job and although she always spent time with William when he was there on a Wednesday or at a weekend, she was always checking her phone for emails or messages and the flat always had lots of important looking papers dotted around.

In fact, William and his mum never ate a meal at the dining table because it was always full of his mum's work things.

"Next time you're here," she would say, but then it was still full the next time and so they sat on the sofa to eat instead. William didn't mind and he enjoyed having tea on his knee, with his mum, watching a film.

They still ate at the table in the kitchen when he was at 'home' with his dad. Home was actually a strange word to use, because William's mum kept on telling him her flat was also William's home, even though it didn't feel like it to him. But he had to be careful not to call his dad's house 'home' as sometimes it made his mum upset. In the end, he called them 'dad's house' and 'mum's flat'.

His dad had changed his job so he had far less work to do and all of it could now be done from his office at home. Although he sometimes had a call to do, or an email to send, most days he could stop work when William came back from school.

William had never spent this much time with his dad and at first, neither of them really knew what to do. For the first few weeks his dad would just sit on the sofa with William and watch TV with him. But William liked watching cartoons and programmes about aliens who went to school with normal kids and after a few minutes of these programmes his dad would start fidgeting. He managed a whole week of just sitting with William and not commenting, although William could tell he wanted to. Eventually he couldn't help himself.

"So, why do they go to school when they know all about the universe already?"

"Is the computer on their ship a bit like an Alexa?"

"Tom and Jerry was always my favourite cartoon when I was your age. Have you watched any Tom and Jerry?"

"Can't the other kids all see the tails the aliens have got?"

"Does anything actually happen in this cartoon?"

They soon decided William would get an hour in front of the TV on his own every day after school and then they would do something together before tea. On most afternoons they went into the garden and practised rugby. William liked those days the best. But they also did jigsaws together, which weren't quite as boring as William first thought, and his dad even taught him a few card games.

After they had spent some time together, William's dad would go off and cook for them. He said something about being 'determined to give his son a home-cooked meal', but sometimes William just wished they could have fish and chips or a Chinese takeaway instead.

His dad was very good at cooking about three different things - William really, really liked his sausage and mash for example - but for some reason he was really, really bad at everything else. William didn't understand how it could work like that, but it definitely did. When William had some homework to do, he would often sit in the kitchen to do it in case he had a question he needed to ask his dad. But soon he just enjoyed sitting there to watch his dad struggle with whatever it was he was trying to cook.

Eventually, his dad got a bit better and the food was actually quite tasty, but he still always made a complete mess of the kitchen with pans and bowls everywhere.

His dad was very good at cleaning though. The house was always so much cleaner now than when his mum had been living there. And no matter how messy the kitchen had been the night before, it was always spotlessly clean the next morning, along with the rest of the house. Again though, William found it very strange his dad could keep the house so clean, but couldn't seem to understand clothes also needed to be cleaned. On the weekends William stayed with his dad, he got into the habit of checking his school uniform every Sunday after lunch and every time he would find it still in the washing basket where he had left it on a Friday and have to remind his dad to wash it.

At school, things just carried on as normal. William was nervous at first about being teased, but it didn't happen at all. Well, it happened once as Stephen tried to make some jokes about William, but Harry punched him and said, "Leave him alone! He's ok." Stephen looked so shocked he stopped and didn't say anything again.

Instead of being teased, William realised plenty of other kids were in a similar situation to him. He talked to Finlay more and got to learn about how he had lived without his dad for two years. And every now and again a girl in his year would tap him on the arm and ask him how he was.

"Fine," was William's usual answer. But one day, Abigail came up to him in the playground and sat down on the bench next to him, as William was waiting for Tom and Finlay.

"I know what you're going through," she said. "My mum and dad split up nearly two years ago."

William didn't know what to say, all he could manage was,

"Oh!"

"I hated it at first, but it's actually pretty good now," Abigail said. "My dad's gone back to Ghana, so I don't see him much, but he sends me loads of photos. He's got a new wife and they've got another daughter, but she's cute, so it's ok."

William still didn't know what to say, so he just nodded. But then Abigail saw Tom and Finlay walking towards them.

"Anyway, you can talk to me if you want," she said as she stood up. As she walked off, she turned round and put her thumb up to William.

Tom and Finlay just grinned at William and all William could do was shrug back at them.

Rugby also carried on as normal. William was picked for some matches, but not others. Mr Giles had told everyone he wanted as many of the boys to play as possible and so he was doing something called 'squad rotation'. William obviously wanted to play, but he also liked being a sub and watching the match.

There was one more cup game before the Christmas holiday and William had been picked as a sub for this match. This one was an easy game. Northbrook were 28-0 ahead by half-time and scored two more quick tries straight after half-time. At that point, Mr Giles made all of his substitutions to allow everyone to have at least some time on the pitch.

With so many new players on all at once, Northbrook didn't play as well, but they did score one more try a few seconds before the end of the match. William had been involved and had played a good pass out to the winger who ran past the opposite winger and scored in the corner. The replacement kicker missed the conversion, but by then it didn't matter as Northbrook won 47-0 anyway. They were now in the cup semi-finals, which would be played after the Christmas holiday.

For William, Christmas was strange. All the usual traditions they normally had as a family couldn't happen this year. Although both his mum and dad tried really hard, Christmas just felt strange.

William's dad had bought a Christmas tree for the house and they had decided to decorate it together, but it started badly as his dad was nearly an hour in the loft looking for where they had stored the decorations. By the time he returned from the loft, he was in a bad mood muttering about, 'she always does this,' and William was already bored.

The combination of his dad's bad mood and William's boredom meant it wasn't long before they were arguing. It wasn't helped by William dropping one of the baubles, accidentally kicking it and smashing it into tiny pieces.

"Oh for Heaven's sake! Can't you be more careful?!" his dad yelled.

"It was an accident! I didn't mean it!" William yelled back.

After William's dad had cleaned up all the broken glass from the bauble, they decided not to decorate the tree together and his dad decorated it all, once William had gone to bed.

William actually preferred the days he spent with his mum over the Christmas holidays. Normally, she would get stressed about Christmas, about the food, the presents, which guests they were having, or where they would need to drive to. She was also the one who organised all the decorations in the house. One day, during the first week of December, William would leave a normal house and go off to school in the morning and return to a Christmas wonderland that afternoon.

But this year, his mum had put a tiny fake tree up in her flat - it was only big enough for one piece of tinsel and four baubles - along with some of the Christmas cards she had received on the bookcase. She told William she wasn't going to bother with any more decorations and that she was planning to have beans on toast for Christmas dinner.

When he got back to his dad's after that visit, he couldn't help but tell him about it. "You'll never guess what mum is doing for Christmas Day," he said.

"Is she going crazy, like normal?"

"No. The opposite. She said she's just going to have beans on toast!"

"Well, that doesn't sound like your mum."

"I know," said William. "I hope she's ok."

As he went to bed that night he could hear his dad on the phone.

"Hi, Fiona, it's Mark. Listen, William told me about your Christmas Day plans..."

In the end, William's mum came round to the house and the three of them had Christmas dinner together. William was really pleased she was coming, but it was probably the most uncomfortable afternoon William had ever experienced, due to the tension in the air as everyone was so determined to enjoy themselves.

His dad cooked the turkey, while his mum had brought round a trifle for dessert. His dad's cooking was actually quite good, but he got his timings all wrong and so some of the meal was cold by the time it was dished up. The hot gravy warmed up all the cold bits of food and the meal itself went well. William's dad had bought some crackers, so they had pulled those and William had insisted they all wear the paper hats during the meal. The jokes in the crackers had been rubbish, but all three of them had forced themselves to awkwardly laugh at them. However, this inspired William's dad to try and tell more of his rubbish jokes while they were eating. It had been hard for William and his mum to force themselves to laugh at those.

One thing which nearly ruined the meal completely was William's dad serving brussel sprouts to his mum; apparently he had forgotten she didn't eat them.

"Mark..." she said as he put a big spoonful of them onto her plate.

"What's up?"

"Don't you remember? I've not been able to eat those since I was pregnant."

"Oh no! Sorry, Fiona, I forgot."

"What's new?" sighed William's mum and William could feel the tension rising again. His mum started to look down at her plate and she looked like might start to cry.

William's dad sighed and started to apologise again. But then he stopped himself.

"Actually, of course I remember. It's just that I had tried to wipe from my mind the memory of the reaction they used to have on you when you were pregnant!"

"Mark!" said William's mum, and she looked up, shocked. William thought this might be the moment the meal ended and his mum went home. For a couple of seconds, he held his breath. Then both of his parents burst out laughing.

William's parents then told William the story of how his mum craved sprouts when she was pregnant with William. However, Brussels sprouts can cause some people to fart and this is what happened to William's mum. It was especially bad at night while she was asleep, according to William's dad. While they were telling the story, they both giggled, which made William laugh too. It also, finally, broke the tension.

After dinner, they had some of the trifle William's mum had brought round, but they were all so full they couldn't eat much. At five o'clock, William's mum decided it was time for her to leave. Once William had closed the door and waved her off his dad let out the biggest sigh William had ever heard.

"Well, that went ok, didn't it, kiddo?" he said to William, but while they were watching the film together his dad drank a whole bottle of red wine on his own.

One good thing about this strange, new Christmas was that William got some great presents, including a new pair of rugby boots and tickets for a real, professional rugby match from his dad, and a membership pass for the zoo from his mum, which meant they could go as often as they liked. However, the best thing about Christmas was when he helped his dad take all the decorations down and it was all over. William felt like he had let out a sigh as loud as his dad's on Christmas Day when the last decoration came down.

William knew it was unusual for him, but he was actually glad the holidays were over. Strangely, he was looking forward to going back to school and having everything back to normal, or at least this new way of being normal they had developed. Over the weeks before the holidays, he had got used to the pattern of spending time at either his mum's flat or his dad's house. His dad was sometimes a bit flustered about the cooking, but William liked seeing more of him. While his mum seemed to be super busy with work, but also more relaxed at the same time.

William would have preferred them to be back living in the same house, then things could go back to the old way of being normal. But he thought maybe, just maybe, he could cope with this new arrangement.

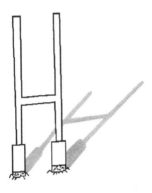

14

In the first few days of the new term, William tried to avoid all the conversations everybody was having about the Christmas holidays. Apart from Christmas Day, which had been quite uncomfortable, he'd enjoyed the holidays more than he had expected to, but he still wasn't ready to chat about his new situation to everyone at school.

He also didn't like talking about presents. Most of the other boys seemed to talk about the latest games console they'd been given for Christmas - William wasn't into games - and he just didn't understand most of the presents the girls talked about.

For the first three days William sat quietly in lessons, and played Top Trumps with Tom and Finlay at break and lunch time. Both Tom and Finlay had been given new Top Trumps sets for Christmas - Tom had received another superhero one and Finlay's was about killer animals.

"My dad knows I like animals, but doesn't really know much else about me," Finlay shrugged, as he got the pack out one day. But it was quite good to play and the three of them soon preferred playing with this set to the superhero one.

On the first Wednesday back at school after Christmas, William walked round to his mum's flat as usual. He buzzed and waited for her to answer. After a few minutes with no answer, he buzzed again.

"What?" came the rather sharp reply through the intercom.

"Oh! Erm... hi, Mum," William said. "It's only me."

"Oh no!" his mum exclaimed. "No, sorry. I didn't mean 'oh no, it's you'. I meant, 'oh no, it's Wednesday'. Look, just come up," and she buzzed the door open.

By the time he'd reached the top of the stairs and knocked on the door to her flat, William's mum was talking on her mobile.

"Yes, Stephen, I can still do the report... Yes, I know, first thing tomorrow... I know... I know... Yes, I understand how important the account is... Look, I said I'll do it and I will... Ok... I've got to go now, but I'll call you back if I've got any problems."

William had taken his jacket off and taken his school bag into his bedroom and now he was sitting on the sofa waiting for his mum to finish her call.

"I'm sorry about that, sweetie," she said as she put the phone down. "I just, I just hadn't realised it was Wednesday. Or, I knew it was Wednesday, but I'd forgotten what it meant. Not that I'd forgotten about you, of course I hadn't. It's... well, I'd forgotten you'd be here."

William sat there looking confused while his mum rambled at him.

His mum took a deep breath to calm herself down and sat next to William and gave him a cuddle.

"I'm sorry," she said again, but now she was speaking a bit slower and more calmly. Then cuddled him again. "Even adults get a bit confused by new systems and routines," she said. "I've got some really important work to do this evening and I'd forgotten Wednesday was our night. So now I've promised I'll do the work which means I'll be extremely busy. I'm going to try and phone your dad and see if he can help out."

She stood up, picked her mobile phone back up and dialled.

"Hi, Mark, it's me," she said as she smiled at William and walked out of the room.

The conversation didn't last long and William couldn't hear all of it, but he could hear the last few things his mum said as she started to talk louder and louder so that she was almost shouting by the end.

"... I know it's my responsibility, I was just asking if you could help..."

"... I don't know, maybe you could support my career for once..."

"... FINE! I'll sort it!"

William's mum opened the door and took a deep breath.

"Well, it turns out your dad's busy tonight as well. I'll text Sharon and see if you could spend some time with Finlay, ok?"

William nodded and put the TV on and his mum went to make herself a coffee and text Finlay's mum.

William's mum sat back at her desk and carried on working while William watched TV. It was the programme about the aliens going to school and it was a funny episode about one of them wanting to be elected onto the student council. William laughed a couple of times and each time his mum glanced over at him. She smiled, but only with her mouth, and then put her head back down to look at her work again.

The TV programme started out as an election campaign but soon turned into a riot in the school, with the aliens leading the revolt. It was really funny and William had to laugh.

All of a sudden, his mum got up from her chair, grabbed the TV remote and turned the TV off.

"I'm sorry! But I've got to concentrate. Can you just... can you just read in your room or something?"

It wasn't fair; it was just getting to the good bit. William dragged himself off the sofa, sighed and went into his room. The book he was reading was at his dad's and he didn't feel like starting a new book, so he just lay down on his bed for a while. He realised he was starting to fall asleep lying there, so he rolled himself up and started to get changed out of his school uniform.

Oh no! he thought, his favourite jeans were at his dad's. For a few minutes William just stood in his room wearing only his pants, he couldn't work out what to do - he wasn't allowed to watch TV, he didn't have his book to read and he couldn't wear his favourite jeans. He wished he was back at his dad's house.

Eventually, he put on a pair of old tracksuit bottoms and flopped back on his bed. After a few minutes of lying there being bored, he decided to look under his bed to see what toys he had here. When his mum had moved she suggested he bring some toys round, but he wasn't sure what he should take. He didn't want to be without his favourite toys when he was at his dad's and anyway, he didn't really play with toys much anymore, he much preferred to watch TV or to read.

Under the bed were some old Lego sets he'd forgotten about. There were two spaceships and a motorbike, all from different sets, but he started to play a game about how they were exploring the surface of a new planet together.

William wasn't sure how long he'd been playing for, when his mum knocked at the door,

"Can I come in?"

"Yeah," William replied, not very enthusiastically.

"So, Sharon can't help out either," his mum said as she sat down on the bed. "And as you know I've got lots of work to do. I'm sorry, but can you just entertain yourself tonight?"

"I suppose," William mumbled, "it's just..."

"I know, I know. Most of your stuff is at your dad's. I've cleared up some of my paperwork so I can work in my room and I've got you a couple of DVDs out. Why don't you watch those while I work, then I'll call for some takeaway pizza in a bit? How's that?"

William nodded.

"Yeah, I think I can manage that," he said.

"Thank you so much, sweetheart," said his mum and gave him a hug. By the time William had come out of his room his mum had already taken her laptop and some of her papers away into her bedroom, so William put a DVD in the machine and settled down to watch the film.

After half an hour, his mum came out of her room to order William a pizza, then after roughly another half an hour, it arrived. William's mum paid the driver and put the pizza onto a plate for William, but then she went back into her room to her work.

William enjoyed the film, but he still felt a bit fed up. He didn't see his mum again that evening, apart from when she told him it was time to go to bed, so he was still fed up and grumpy in the morning as he set off to go to school.

William's mum apologised again to him in the morning, but he just shrugged and carried on eating his breakfast. By the time he set off to school, she was already on her laptop so just offered William a quick wave to say goodbye.

$$O \quad O \quad O$$

That weekend William was with his dad. They had kept the tradition of getting a Chinese takeaway on a Friday night, so William had his favourite fried rice and chicken with cashew nuts. On Saturday, his dad had said he wanted to clean the whole house, so William spent most of the day reading and playing in his room. He liked it when he was able to help his dad, so he did one or two jobs with him: they stripped the sheets off the bed and put the new, cleans ones on, and tidied up in the garage together.

His dad had said he wanted to move some things up into the loft as well, so he'd want a hand from William later. William didn't like going into the dark loft, which was full of cobwebs, but he was happy to hold the ladder and to pass things up to his dad.

William turned over the last page of his book, he'd loved reading it and hadn't expected the twist at the end. He couldn't wait to start the next one in the series. However, as he put the book down, he realised it was getting dark outside and he wondered when they might be having their tea. He also realised he'd promised to help take things up to the loft.

He got off his bed and went downstairs.

"Dad, you ok? Did you need some help from me?"

When he got downstairs, his dad was sitting at the dining table with boxes of photos scattered across the table. His eyes were red and he wiped his hand across his face as William entered.

"Alright there, Champ?" he said as he saw William. "I was just looking at some old photos. Look, here are some of you as a baby." And he handed a box to William.

William had seen a few of these before; there was one he recognised - it was in a frame on the wall at his grandparents' house. William was in a bed in hospital and both his mum and his dad were standing at the end of the bed, grinning. William remembered being told this was the morning after he was born, just before they left the hospital with him.

William's dad pointed out a couple of photos of William pulling funny faces as a baby.

"I think you were doing a poo in your nappy when we took that photo!" he said, trying to make William laugh.

"What are these ones here?" asked William as he had seen a box on the floor by his dad's feet.

"Oh, nothing. Don't worry about it," his dad replied.

"Can I have a look?" asked William as he bent down to the box.

"I SAID NO!" He scooped up the box just as William was bending down, catching William across the face with the corner of the box as he lifted it up.

"Ow!" William clutched his face and sat down on the floor, looking up at his dad.

"I told you not to touch it," was all his dad could say to him and he turned his back on William, hugging the box tightly to his chest. William stood up and silently went upstairs to his bedroom.

Once he was upstairs, William had a look at his face in the mirror. The skin wasn't cut, but there was a red mark where the box had scratched him. He sat on his bed and didn't know what to feel. He was angry and upset with his dad, but he was also worried. Is this what is was going to be like from now on? His dad getting angry and his mum forgetting about him?

After about ten minutes there was a knock at his bedroom door.

"Can I come in?"

"S'pose so," William reluctantly replied.

"I'm really, really sorry," his dad said. "Let's have a look... just a scratch, that's good." He went to give William a hug, but then stopped himself when he saw William back away slightly. "I don't know what else to

169

say," he said standing back up, "so... I'll sort some food out now, I guess." And with that his dad walked out of William's room.

William watched him leave and felt strange. It was as if his dad had no energy at all and this left William with no energy either. William sat on his bed, unsure of what to do. He didn't want to follow his dad and thought it would be best to let him be on his own for a while. But he couldn't be bothered to start a new book, or play with any of his toys. Instead, he decided to lie down on his bed for a few minutes until he had some inspiration. Soon he was fast asleep.

He wasn't sure what time it was when he woke up, but it was dark outside and he was hungry. He couldn't hear any noise coming from downstairs so he went down to find his dad. William assumed his dad would be in the kitchen cooking, so he tried there first, but the light was off and there were no sounds.

He switched the light on and saw his dad sat at the kitchen table. The box of photos was next to him and so was a bottle of wine and a glass with some wine in.

His dad blinked at the light and looked up at William.

"Hi there, kiddo," he said, as he poured more wine into his glass.

"What are we having for tea, dad? I'm starving."

"What? Oh yeah. Um... I dunno. I came in to cook something, but then I fancied a glass of wine and then... Oh well." His dad grinned, but only with his mouth.

His eyes still looked like they had done upstairs in William's room, as if they, and the rest of his body, had no energy in them at all.

"Beans on toast will work for you, won't it?"

"Sure, Dad."

A couple of minutes later and William was sitting at the kitchen table with a plate of beans in front of him.

"Are you not having any?" he asked his dad.

"I'm not hungry right now," his dad replied as he poured more wine into his glass.

It only took William a couple of minutes to eat the beans on toast and then he helped himself to another slice of toast, but with jam on this time.

After he had finished, he sat quietly for a couple of minutes. His dad was just staring at the closed box of photographs, not saying anything.

"Um, Dad, are you...?"

His dad suddenly sat upright, looked at William, smiled and said,

"Right! Finished? All ok?" William just nodded. "Good lad! Time for bed, I think. You can read for a bit once you're in bed, but not too long. Give me a hug now and I'll tidy up the kitchen."

William stood up and cautiously went to hug his dad, but his dad just pulled him in and hugged him a bit tighter and longer than usual.

"Ok, kiddo. Good night, sleep well," he ruffled William's hair as he stood up and began to clear away the plates William had used.

William went upstairs and got ready for bed. He thought after his earlier snooze he wouldn't be tired enough to go to sleep, so he got into bed with a new book and settled down for a long read, but within only two pages the book had fallen onto the bed and William had fallen fast asleep.

When he woke up in the morning, it was light outside and his bedside clock said 8:37. He rolled over and the book fell off the bed with a thud which gave him a shock, but he decided he'd read a bit more before he got up. As he read, he realised he couldn't remember anything he had read last night, so he just started from the beginning and read to the end of the first chapter. By the time he had finished the chapter, it was 9:04, so he thought it was time to get up and have some breakfast.

At first, he wondered whether his dad might be cooking some breakfast for him. He sometimes did at the weekends. His bacon sandwiches were lovely, however his pancakes needed a bit more work. But, as he went downstairs, he couldn't hear any cooking sounds or smell any cooking smells.

He opened the kitchen door and was surprised to see the light was on already. There was no sign of his dad in the kitchen, but there was an empty bottle of wine on the kitchen table where his dad had been sitting last night.

What was even stranger though was that the pan and plates from William's tea last night were still dirty next to the kitchen sink.

William wondered if his dad was poorly, so he went back upstairs to his bedroom to see if he was ok. He knocked and opened the bedroom door.

"Dad, are you ok?" he said as he tiptoed in. But once the door was open wide enough, he could see there was no one in the bed and the bed was still made, as if it hadn't been slept in at all.

William was worried now. He ran back downstairs and checked the rest of the house to see where his dad could be. As he burst into the sitting room, there was his dad asleep on the sofa.

"Dad! Dad! Are you ok?" asked William giving him a shake.

"Leave me alone," his dad mumbled.

But William just shook him again. "Come on! It's morning," he said. William's dad sat bolt upright, looked at William straight in the eyes,

"LEAVE! ME! ALONE!" he yelled and then lay back on the sofa, closed his eyes and went back to sleep.

William jumped back and as he did he kicked over another nearly empty bottle of wine. Nearly empty, apart from the little bit of wine which now dribbled onto the carpet.

William didn't know what to do with himself, so he picked up the wine bottle and took it into the kitchen.

Then he went back with a cloth to try and wipe up the spilt wine. He just seemed to be making a bigger patch of mess though, and his dad was snoring loudly next to him as he wiped. So he stopped and went into the kitchen to get himself some Cheerios for breakfast instead.

After his breakfast, William still wasn't sure what to do. He went upstairs and sat on his bed reading for a while, but he couldn't really concentrate on the words, so he decided to put his rugby kit on and throw the ball around in the garden. As he went back downstairs he thought he'd ask his dad if he wanted to join him.

His dad was still snoring on the sofa, but William shook him awake again.

"Oh, for Pity's sake! What now?"

"Do you want to play some rugby with me?"

"No. I just... no," his dad said without even opening his eyes properly.

"But I thought..."

"I SAID NO!" This time his dad had opened his eyes and he was staring right at William and it frightened William. "Go on! Get lost!" he said, this time a bit more gently and he had dropped his eyes to look at the floor instead.

His dad closed his eyes and lay back down on the sofa. He turned his back to William and said, "Just leave me alone." Quietly, he started to cry. William could see his body shake with the crying so he bent down and put his arm around his dad. His dad shook William's arm off and rolled over again on the sofa. "Just go!"

William picked up his rugby ball and ran out into the garden, he threw the ball up into the air but he couldn't catch it as his eyes were full of tears, making the ball just a blur. When it came down again, he completely missed it with his hands and it hit his foot and rolled away under the shrubs.

"Great! Just what I need!" he said to himself as he knelt down to try and find it.

"Hurry up and put your boots on, Billy, and stop messing around!"

William looked down and it wasn't a rugby ball in his hand, but a boot. He stood up and he was no longer in his back garden. He was in a changing room and the lights were being turned off.

"Come on!" the voice said. "Kick-off is soon and we still need to get warmed up." And a face disappeared behind the door leaving William alone. He looked down and he was in full rugby kit, all except for the one boot in his hands.

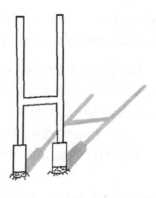

15

Billy put his boots on as quickly as he could and ran out of the changing room to join the rest of the team. They were only just ahead of him, so they hadn't started their warm-up routine yet.

"Finally! Come on, slow coach!" called one of the coaches. There were a few ironic cheers and claps from the younger members of the team.

"Ok, enough of that. Let's get the warm-up started. You know what to do. Off you go."

All the players set off to run across the pitch from side to side and Billy followed them. They went across the pitch like that, just gentle jogging, three times until they were at the far side of the pitch. On the fourth time across, instead of jogging normally they side-stepped. The fifth time they side-stepped facing the other way and on the sixth time they ran flicking their heels up to their bottoms.

After the jogging, they all stood around in a semi-circle and did some stretches. One of the players, Billy thought it was the captain, stood in front and called out what they had to do. They worked their way up the body from the feet, heels, calves, all the way up to the neck and then back down again with different stretches.

Next came a few sprints. A full sprint to halfway across the pitch, followed by a gentle jog back. Then it was a sprint with a high knee lift, followed by a backwards sprint, which was funny because a couple of the players fell over, and finally a couple more normal sprints.

Billy was one of the fastest players, so he didn't have to sprint flat out, but he was still breathing hard by the end. During one of the jogs back to the start, Billy glanced over to the other side of the pitch and saw the other team, Billy thought he'd heard someone call them Burford, doing something similar. They weren't doing exactly the same as his team, but you could tell they were warming up too.

After the sprints, the team split into two. Billy was pulled aside by one of the younger players and he joined in with their group. Billy didn't want to be rude, but he couldn't help noticing nearly every player in the other group was a lot fatter, or at least bigger, than the ones in his group. It was pretty obvious they had been split into forwards and backs and that Billy was a back.

The forwards were doing scrum practice, as well as rucks and mauls. When they'd finished, they did some line out practice.

Billy's group passed the ball to each other and practised running across the pitch, including the special move Billy had practised with them where he ran into the line of players from a different angle. After a few minutes, one of the coaches started kicking the ball high into the air and each player had to run up and catch the ball. Billy dropped his first go and his heart was in his mouth straight away, but he had two more attempts before the practice was over and he caught both of those.

A whistle sounded and both teams ran back into the changing rooms. Billy's team all sat down once they were in there and the coach read out the team. Billy was named as a sub and at first, he felt relieved, but then disappointed. He was sure he could do this, he'd been as good as anyone else during the warm-up.

With the team announced, new rugby shirts were handed out with everyone's number on the back. Everyone got changed and then put a tracksuit top over their shirt.

They all stood and Billy assumed they were going out onto the pitch when the captain called them all together.

All the players gathered into a big huddle in the centre of the changing room and Billy could smell a strange mixture of sweat, fabric conditioner from the clean shirts, ointments and sprays which the players had put onto injuries and, on top of all that, he was sure a couple of the players had farted as well. It smelt like men, and he wanted to giggle, but everyone was looking very serious, so he managed to keep a straight face.

"This is it, lads," the captain said. He was almost shouting, but not quite, just talking very loudly. He wasn't telling them off, but he did look everyone in the eye as he spoke. Many of the players subtly nodded back to him as he looked at them.

"We've got to want it... Want it more than them... Hit them hard, do it early... Win your personal battle, make sure they know they're in for a fight... Then we've got to execute... Be aggressive, but in control... We know we can do this... So let's B****Y do it!"

The last sentence was a shout. In fact, he'd got a bit louder with every sentence until at the end he was shouting at everyone. The last sentence had included a swear word as well and Billy was shocked, but all the other players were nodding, shouting, stamping their boots on the floor and slapping each other on the back.

As they ran out, a few of the players yelled and whooped and then they were out on the pitch.

From the changing rooms, the players ran about 20 paces forwards and down a gentle slope to the pitch. As they came down the slope, they were almost at the half-way line and Billy's team turned left. At that end of the pitch, behind the posts, there was a hedge, a narrow road and then some trees on the edge of a large field.

At the other end of the pitch was a high fence with houses behind it. On the side of the pitch nearest to the changing room there were two curved, Perspex shelters, which were the 'benches'. Billy's coach put down the big bag he was carrying and someone else put down some water bottles. On the opposite side of the pitch were some spectators - probably about 40 or 50 people who had chosen to come down and watch the rugby on a Saturday afternoon.

Just before the match kicked off, the players took off their tracksuit tops and Billy and the other substitutes had to run round and collect them. The players were so focused they almost didn't see Billy as he took their tops. They were staring ahead at the opposition team. You could almost see the moves or tackles in their eyes as they rehearsed them in their mind.

Then the match started; it was played at a frantic pace. Northbrook seemed to start the stronger; they spent much of the first five minutes in the opposition's half and had several minutes of possession.

Billy spent his time watching the centres play. Both of them looked older, but they were still very fit and fast. There was one move which amazed Billy. Northbrook had won a scrum in the centre of the pitch about 30 metres from the opposition try line. The backs had been split into two lines, either side of the scrum, with the two centres and a winger on the side of the pitch closest to Billy.

As the ball came out of the scrum, the scrum half took two steps to his right, towards this side of the pitch. As he did so the inside centre started moving to his right. The scrum half threw a long pass, missing out the inside centre and passed to the outside centre. He took a few paces forward and passed it out to the winger. He set off to sprint, but was soon covered. Just when he was about to be tackled, the inside centre suddenly appeared again on his inside. The winger passed and the centre was through the line and only a few metres away from scoring a try.

Billy, as well as the rest of the crowd jumped up in excitement, but just before the try line, the opposition scrambled back and the Northbrook centre was engulfed in a crowd of players. Eventually, the opposition won the ball back and it was kicked clear. There was no score, but Billy was amazed at the skill on show.

Only a few minutes later however, disaster struck the Northbrook team. They lost possession near the opposition try line and the opposing full back kicked the ball clear. However, it didn't go out into touch and instead bounced infield. The Northbrook team had to turn and chase, but the Burford full back was quicker. He raced up the touchline, kicked the ball ahead again and continued running. He was inside the Northbrook twenty-two when he picked the ball up and ran to the try line. At the last minute, the Northbrook full back, who had run the whole length of the pitch, dived to attempt a try saving tackle. Unfortunately, he missed and the try was scored.

What was even worse though, worse than being seven points down (Burford had managed to kick the conversion), was the Northbrook full back caught a boot in the face as he had tried to make the last-ditch tackle. It was a complete accident, but it caused his nose to bleed. The first-aider rushed on and tried to stop the blood while the conversion was being taken, but it was no good – he was going to have to come off.

The coach leaned over to where the subs were watching the game,

"Billy, get your top off. You're on!"

Billy was too shocked to say anything.

"Right, blood replacement. Steve, move to full back. Billy will go outside centre," the coach shouted across to the team.

"Come on then, lad. On you go," he said as he turned and saw that Billy had hardly moved.

Billy quickly stripped off his tracksuit top, checked his boots were laced up, fiddled with his shorts for a second, took a deep breath and ran onto the pitch. The coach patted his back as he ran on and said something about 'focus' and 'hit hard', but Billy didn't really hear him.

Because Northbrook had conceded a try, it was their kick-off, but Billy was still in shock and ran to the posts, just as the rest of the team was running up to the halfway line.

"Oi, Billy! Over here, son!" The Northbrook inside centre called him over and pointed to his left to where Billy should stand. "He's tricky, but he always wants to step to his left, so you can line him up and hit him hard," the centre continued.

As he was talking, Billy took a long look at him. He was about 35, with short, almost shaved hair which was starting to slowly leave the top of his head altogether. His face looked like leather, tough and cracked in places. He looked like he wanted to kill Billy, there was an anger in his eyes, but Billy could see laughter lines too.

"Got it?"

It took Billy a moment before he realised he was talking about the man Billy was supposed to mark, the outside centre on the opposition team.

"Yeah, yeah. His left."

Then the kick-off was taken, and Billy and the rest of the Northbrook team charged after the ball.

After only a few seconds Billy was caught up in a ruck, supporting the winger as he was tackled. He didn't quite know how, but he remembered to stay on his feet and not dive in. He helped form the ruck and suddenly the forwards arrived and secured the ball. He got knocked to the ground and rolled away just as the ball was being passed out, but someone gave him a friendly pat on the head as he got to his feet.

The ball seemed to go back and forth all around Billy without him ever touching it for what felt like hours but could only have been a few minutes. Billy had barely caught his breath from the shock of going onto the pitch, but he seemed to keeping up with everything.

After a period of defending, Northbrook kicked the ball forwards, but it went straight to the opposition full back, who managed to pick it up and kick it away before the Northbrook team even had chance to chase properly. As the ball flew up in the air someone had shouted "Billy!"

Billy looked around and realised the kick was coming straight for him. He glanced to his left and right, but couldn't see a teammate. He gulped. He could feel himself starting to sweat. He took three paces back to get himself in the right position and looked up at the falling ball.

It seemed to take forever to fall. Out of the corner of his eye he could see opposition players running towards him. They were big. Very big. He gulped again. Then he looked up again and realised he was in slightly the wrong position - the ball was in danger of going over his head. Another step back and a step to his left and then the ball was there. He had it. It was in his hands. Then, it wasn't.

He heard the groan before he felt the hit. As he was on the ground he heard the whistle. He'd dropped the ball, but the opposition player had tackled him anyway.

By nearly catching the ball, but letting it bounce off him and hit the ground, Billy had 'knocked on', which meant the opposition team would have a scrum and the chance to win the ball back. However, Billy had also been tackled after he'd dropped the ball. In rugby, you are only allowed to be tackled when you have the ball and so this had been a 'late tackle'. A late tackle was a more serious offence than a knock on, so instead of giving away a scrum, Billy had won a penalty. The Northbrook stand off kicked the ball into touch near the opposition try line, creating a Northbrook line out and a chance for a try.

Before the line out was taken, he heard his name called from the sideline. He ignored it at first as he thought he was going to be told off for dropping the ball, but he glanced over the third time he heard his name called. The coach was waving him over and the injured full back was ready to come back on the pitch.

Billy went over to the sideline, put his tracksuit top back on and joined the rest of the substitutes. He was exhausted and he'd only been on the pitch for seven minutes.

Northbrook scored a try from the line out. The forwards had won the ball and formed a maul which saw them march across the opposition line. They had put the ball down near the edge of the pitch, so it made for a tricky conversion, but the Northbrook Number 10 had kicked it with ease and the scores were level again.

However, even though the try scoring move had taken less than a couple of minutes, the Northbrook full back had come off the pitch again. He hadn't touched the ball or been tackled, but he was complaining of feeling 'wobbly' as he called it. It was clear the head injury was more serious than just a nosebleed.

"Right, Billy, you're on again," the coach has said.

"Steve, back to full back. Ref, permanent swap this time please."

It seemed to Billy that he had only just put his top back on when he was taking it off again. He took a couple more deep breaths and ran back onto the pitch. This time he knew where he was going and joined in with his teammates as they got ready to receive the kick-off.

Fortunately, no high kicks came over to Billy and the rest of the half seemed to flash by in a blur. Billy had been passed the ball a few times. Once he'd passed it out to the winger on his outside and had almost set up a try, but the winger had been tackled into touch a couple of metres away from the try line. Another time he'd been passed the ball just as one of the opposition forwards clattered into him. He'd ended up at the bottom of a pile of players, but had remembered to roll over to face his team and had worked hard to release the ball and lay it back.

On another occasion, he'd had to sprint back and tackle his opposite number who had made a break. He'd manage to reach him and tackle him as hard as he could, forcing the other player to drop the ball, giving away a knock on and a scrum to Northbrook.

Northbrook had scored two more tries in this time. The first was great work by the forwards again as they had managed to win a scrum near the opposition try line.They had pushed them back in the scrum so that the Northbrook Number 8 had touched the ball down for the try. The second involved an interception by the Northbrook full back. The opposition had been a bit too adventurous just inside their own half. The scrum half had tried a long pass straight out to the winger, missing out two players. Northbrook's full back had read it perfectly, intercepted it and ran towards the line. About ten metres out, he'd passed it to the winger on his right. In the end, it was an easy try.

One of the conversions had been missed, but it didn't matter as Burford had only managed a penalty in reply, so at half-time it was 19-10 to Northbrook.

Billy sat in the changing rooms at half-time and it took all his effort for him not to throw up. He'd been fine while he was playing but now he realised just how hard he was breathing. He took a sip of the sports drink which someone passed to him, but it just made things worse as it was so sweet.

The coach was talking to the team, but all Billy could hear was the blood pumping around his head. He took some deep breaths and another mouthful of the drink and he started to feel better.

"Keep it tight"... "Got this"... "Concentrate"... "Tricky winger"... "Bind tight in the scrum".

Billy had barely caught his breath before everyone was standing up and it was time to go out again for the second half. Just as Billy was leaving the changing room, the inside centre caught up with him.

"You doing ok, son?" he asked.

"Yeah, just needed to catch my breath."

"You're playing well," Jack said. Billy had learnt his name was Jack during the first half.

"Thanks, Jack."

"Remember what I said about when he goes to his left. But if you get chance, you've got the skill to beat him, so have a go."

Billy didn't get the chance to reply as they were already back on the pitch and the ref was blowing the whistle to call the teams to their positions.

The second half started with tackles flying in from all over. Both teams were keen to make sure they came out on top and so the intensity of the match was higher than Billy had ever felt before.

At one stage, Billy had been fed the ball near the wing and could see the try line ahead of him. He'd set off running as fast as he could, but before he'd taken more than five steps he was flattened by a tackle which took him into touch and meant that Burford had a line out and possession of the ball. He hadn't even seen the person who tackled him!

However, Billy also managed to get a few tackles of his own in as well. He found he enjoyed the physical contact and the challenge of tackling and bringing down some of the bigger players. At one point he tackled one of the Burford prop forwards and he was enormous. He was about as tall as Billy, but looked twice as wide and if Billy was going to be a bit rude, he looked like he'd eaten someone the size of Billy as well! He couldn't run very quickly, but he kept moving forward and a couple of the Northbrook players had already bounced off him.

Billy had seen what was happening and had moved inside to tackle him. As he went low to grab his legs, he too seemed to bounce off the prop's thighs, but he managed to grab enough of his ankle to unbalance him and he slowly fell to the ground like a baby rhino learning to walk.

Ten minutes into the second half and Burford scored another try. A penalty on the half-way line had been kicked into touch and from the line out the forwards had created a maul which had slowly marched the ball towards the try line. The maul had been brought down just before the line, but the scrum half was the first to react and had scored just to the left of the posts.

It was a good try and an easy conversion. Seven more points and suddenly Burford were only two points behind Northbrook, with the score at 19-17.

Northbrook tried hard and from what Billy could see they seemed to be playing well, but they didn't have any clear scoring chances for the next ten minutes of play. It seemed as if whatever they attempted, the ball just bounced the wrong way. It bounced into touch when Northbrook didn't want it to, but then didn't when they did. The Burford full back even managed to slip over while chasing back for the ball against Northbrook's winger, but as he slipped the ball bounced up into his hands and he was able to get up and run back up the pitch before the winger could readjust.

After the period of good play, but bad luck, Northbrook were still leading 19-17, but then things went wrong. Another failed attack resulted in a Burford scrum inside their own twenty two. They won the scrum and kept the ball with the forwards. Play after play they managed to keep bringing the ball forward, slowly bringing it up the pitch. They were steady, consistent and in control and the Northbrook forwards couldn't do anything to stop them.

Bit by bit they advanced. Up to the half-way line and another ruck, a pass to one the flankers and he made two or three more metres and yet another ruck was formed.

Again and again they did this and soon they were just outside the Northbrook 22.

Suddenly, the play changed. This time from the ruck the Burford scrum half kicked the ball along the ground behind the Northbrook defensive line. Steve, the replacement Northbrook full back, was caught out of position and the Burford winger collected the ball and ran in to score. He also managed to touch down directly under the posts to make it an even easier conversion. From leading 19-10 at half-time, suddenly Northbrook were 19-24 behind and there were fewer than fifteen minutes of the match left.

As the conversion was being taken, the Northbrook captain called the team together for a team talk.

'Let's focus, lads, we've been asleep this half so far."

"We need more intensity all over the pitch. Line up your man and beat him. Hit him hard in the tackle and let him know that we're better."

"Come on, let's get 'em!"

The last bit was shouted at full volume and the team ran up the pitch to take the kick-off.

There was only about ten minutes of the match left by now, yet Northbrook just couldn't get out of their own half. The try had energised Burford and they had their best period of the match. They had wave after wave of attack; Billy wasn't sure how Northbrook had stopped them from scoring another try. He managed to take a breather as a scrum was being set up and Billy realised he hadn't touched the ball since the try had been scored. In fact, apart from the early run down the wing, he wasn't sure he'd touched it at all in the second half. Yet, he was exhausted.

The Burford scrum was just inside the Northbrook half and once again they seemed to be in control of everything. The scrum half fed the ball in and Burford held the scrum with the ball at the number eight's feet. Billy could see how hard the Northbrook forwards were pushing, but nothing was happening.

"Here we go again," thought Billy.

The ball came out of the scrum and was passed down the Burford line until Billy's opposite number had the ball in hand. He ran at Billy. Billy wasn't sure what to do next, but then he remembered Jack's advice about the player always wanting to go to his left. Billy steadied himself, tackled him hard and low, bringing the player down - causing him to drop the ball for a knock on as he fell. It was a Northbrook scrum!

"Great tackle, Billy!" said one of the forwards as he came over to get ready for the scrum, while a couple of the other forwards slapped Billy on the shoulders.

Would this be the turning point for Northbrook's luck? It didn't seem like it at the time.

From the scrum, Northbrook fed the ball out to Steve, the fullback. As he was inside his own 22, he kicked for touch. However, the kick wasn't quite long enough to go straight out, it landed just inside the touchline and because of the funny shape of a rugby ball, it bounced backwards and back into the pitch. The Burford full back was able to pick it up and steady himself. The ball was now between Burford's twenty two and the half-way line. The full back decided to kick it back deep into the Northbrook half, but as he did his foot slipped and he sliced his kick; it went straight out of play. Suddenly, Northbrook had a line out inside the Burford half and a chance to attack.

The Northbrook forwards won the line out and kept the ball amongst themselves as they slowly moved forward from ruck to ruck. Inside the Burford 22, they were still in control and slowly moving forward.

Billy knew there could only be a couple of minutes left and he could feel the tension and the urgency in every player on the Northbrook team.

Without any warning, the Northbrook tactics changed and the scrum half picked up the ball from the back of the ruck and launched it out to his left. The stand off caught the ball and passed it on all within a fraction of a second. The ball was now with the inside centre, just to Billy's right. He took two paces forwards and passed to his left - to Billy.

Billy knew what was expected of him, he could hear Steve, the full back, to his left calling for the ball and the winger beyond him. Billy should pass the ball left and hope the winger could squeeze past his marker and score a try. But Billy also knew that Burford expected it too, in fact his opposite number had already taken half a step to his right to cover the pass he thought Billy was going to make.

Billy took a step forward and moved his arms across his body from right to left, but instead of letting go and completing the pass, he brought his arms and the ball back into his chest. At the same time, he pushed off hard on his left leg and changed the direction he was running so that he was now running into the gap between the Burford players on his right. The opposition centre was stranded, covering the pass Billy never made, which meant Billy could see the try line only eight metres in front of him. He sprinted and although he could feel a tackle coming in, his momentum took him over the line and he touched the ball down. He had done it! He had scored the winning try!

The Northbrook stand off kicked the conversion while Billy and his teammates were celebrating the try. The whistle to end the match was blown straight after the kick. Northbrook had won and it was thanks to Billy.

Billy was engulfed by his teammates and he fell to the ground as the cheers were ringing in his ears. As Billy was enjoying the moment, the elation of victory and the delight of his teammates, he closed his eyes and laughed at the bottom of the pile of players.

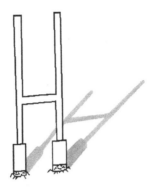

16

William came to, lying on his back in the garden. He was smiling to himself and it felt like he had a heavy weight on him. As he opened his eyes, he saw a big branch was somehow on top of him. He brushed it off, stood up and went back inside.

He helped himself to another bowl of cereal for his lunch so he didn't have to disturb his dad again. He sat quietly in the kitchen eating, thinking about rugby, Billy, dummy passes and scoring tries.

When he had finished, he went upstairs and sat on his bed reading, although it was hard to concentrate on the book as he was still thinking about rugby. Every so often, he would stop reading and practise making a dummy pass with his book acting as a rugby ball.

After about an hour of reading, he heard his dad slowly come upstairs and go into his room. Then William heard his dad turn the shower on. He seemed to be in the shower for a long time, but eventually William could hear his dad walking around his bedroom. He assumed he was getting dressed.

After a few minutes, there was a knock at William's door and his dad walked in and sat next to him on the bed.

"I'm sorry about this morning," he said. He was sat next to William, but he was staring straight ahead not looking at him. His shoulders were slumped and he looked beaten.

"I shouldn't have taken it out on you. None of this is your fault." He turned to face William but stared at the top of his head as if he still couldn't look at him. "It's just, well if I'm honest it's sometimes just really hard for me." He sighed and looked William straight in the eyes. "But it's not your fault."

William could see the tears starting to well up in his dad's eyes and so he gave him a big hug. He didn't quite know what to say. He wanted to tell him how shocked and scared he'd been, how worried he'd been, how he didn't want to have to eat breakfast cereal for lunch every day, but none of that seemed appropriate right now.

"It's ok," he said finally.

"Thank you," said his dad, still hugging William.

They stayed like that in silence for a few more seconds before William's dad pulled away. He wiped his eyes, sat up straight and looked directly at William. He looked like his dad again and not like a scared little boy.

"Ok, I'm gonna make it up to you and cook a great tea."

"Oh!" said William. "Erm..."

"Are you saying my cooking wouldn't be making it up to you?"

William didn't know what to say - he didn't want to upset his dad again - but he wasn't sure his dad's cooking was the right answer.

"It's ok," his dad said starting to laugh. "I agree with you. Chippy instead, then?" William just hugged him again.

$\circ$ $\circ$ $\circ$

William was looking forward to the team being announced for the cup semi-final. He really wanted to play and was excited to be part of the team.

There was one more match first which wasn't part of the cup. Mr Giles had told everyone they would all play some part of the match and then he would pick his best team for the semi-final and the final if they got that far.

The match was on Friday and William was picked to play outside centre. Alex was playing inside centre and Mr Giles had told them to make sure they worked together. William felt as if Mr Giles was telling them he wanted to pick them both for the semi-final, but he couldn't be sure. But even thinking about it made William realise just how nervous he was and how much he wanted to play in the semi-final.

He knew it was important to play well in this match and it meant that for the first few minutes William struggled to concentrate. Twice Alex had to shout at him to make sure he was standing in the right position.

After about ten minutes, the opposition had a break. Northbrook had kicked the ball forward and chased after it, but the opposition had picked it up and started to run it back. The forwards had not chased the kick very well as a group, so there were gaps for the opposition to run through.

William should have chased harder and been further up the pitch, but he hadn't been concentrating, so he was only at the half-way line. He heard Alex yell at him and looked up to see three opposition players running at him. The one in the middle had the ball and was running straight at William.

William wasn't sure what to do, but he knew there was only the full back behind him and if he let all three players get past him they were bound to score. So, he decided to tackle the player in the middle no matter what.

William crouched slightly to get into the best position to tackle and let the opposition player run at him. Just then he looked to pass to his left and William twitched to go right, but it was a dummy pass and he brought the ball back into his chest. However, he'd made the move too early and William had time to reset himself and then bring the attacker crashing to the floor with a powerful tackle. The ball spilled forward and the referee blew his whistle for a Northbrook scrum.

His teammates ran up and congratulated William on his try-saving tackle and Harry even gave him a high five. That woke William up and he was able to concentrate on this match for the rest of the first half.

At the end of the half, William even managed to score a try. A long period of possession had seen Northbrook pass the ball from one side of the pitch to the other and back again. By the time the ball came to William for the second time, the opposition were completely out of position and so with nobody in front of him, William was able to run forward and put the ball down over the try line.

As he had promised to do, Mr Giles changed things around in the second half, although instead of taking William off, he asked if he would play full back instead.

"Well... ok," William replied slowly, "but I don't really..."

"Don't worry, you'll be fine," Mr Giles told him and continued to explain the rest of his changes to the team.

The opposition kicked off for the second half and the ball came straight towards William. It seemed to be in the air for a long time and William was able to get himself into the right position. But at the last minute he panicked, took his eye off the ball and so the first thing he did in his new position as full back was drop the ball, knock on and give away a scrum. Fortunately, Northbrook won the scrum and were able to clear the ball. The forwards started to carry the ball forward and as William stood next to Alex in the line to receive the ball, Alex just looked at him and said,

"Shouldn't you be back there? You know, full back."

"Oh, yeah. Thanks."

William realised he didn't know what to do at full back and then, because he was worrying about where to play, he was making things even worse.

After a few more minutes there was a big kick from the opposition into the Northbrook half. William was standing on the other wing and had to run all the way across the pitch to chase after it. But just as he got there, the opposition winger beat him to it. William launched himself and tackled him hard, but the winger had managed to pass the ball to his teammate who had supported him and he was able to run in for an easy try.

They kicked the conversion as well and although Northbrook were still in the lead, it was much closer now. Before the game kicked off again, Mr Giles made some more substitutions and this time he did bring William off.

"Well played, William," Mr Giles said as William walked by him.

"I'm sorry about that try," William said. "It's just..."

"Their winger's pretty speedy isn't he?" chuckled Mr Giles as he turned away from William to watch the rest of the match.

William was distraught. He had let the opposition score a try. Not only that, but Mr Giles had then substituted him immediately after it. Did this mean he wouldn't be picked for the semi-final? He sat down on the floor and just sighed to himself. A couple of the other players tried to chat to him, but he wasn't really listening. Then he heard one of them say,

"William, isn't that your mum over there?"

William looked up and his mum was standing on the other side of the pitch and she gave a little wave as William looked at her. He got up and ran around to her.

"Did you see that? I was rubbish. I'll never be picked now." William was trying hard not to cry. What he wanted was to let his mum hug him while he cried into her arms, but he thought it would only make things worse, so he stood next to her and faced the game, although he wasn't concentrating on it.

"Hang on a minute," said his mum. "What I saw was you score a great try and make a really good tackle. I know I don't really understand rugby, but I thought you played well."

"Yeah, but their try..." said William and continued to sulk. William's mum didn't say any more and they both watched the rest of the match in silence.

In the end, Northbrook won easily. The try William was blaming himself for was the only one the opposition scored, while Northbrook ran in two more in the second half. When the whistle blew, William ran onto the pitch and sullenly joined his teammates as they jubilantly walked towards Mr Giles.

Both teams shouted out three cheers for each other and shook hands and then Northbrook gathered around Mr Giles.

"Well played, everyone!" he said. "Some of you played in different positions and other than one or two mishaps, I thought you were excellent. Now off you go. Collect all the flags and balls and go and get changed."

Oh no, thought William, 'one or two mishaps' was definitely about me. There's no way I'll be picked for the semi-final. Almost as a punishment to himself, he decided to go and collect the flag in the farthest corner and set off to jog towards it.

However, after only a couple of steps he could feel Harry run past him.

"Race you!" Harry shouted as he ran past. So, William set off running after him. Even with a few paces head start, William was able to easily overtake Harry.

"Right," said William, deciding to be brave, "as I won the race, you've got to carry the flag."

Harry just laughed,

"No problem."

"You played well," said Harry as they were walking across the pitch.

"I was rubbish as full back," said William. "There's no way I'll play the semi."

"Oh shut up! Gilesy doesn't want you to play full back anyway. You'll definitely be picked. Let's have another race. Bet you can't beat me to the changing rooms."

"You're on," said William and set off ahead of Harry. But Harry used the flag to trip William up and leave him in the mud on the pitch. Harry ran past laughing and even William had to laugh a bit as he pulled himself up.

School was boring for William over the next few weeks, as all he could think about was rugby and whether he'd be picked for the semi-final.

They had all the same lessons as before, but William struggled to pay attention to some of them. However, he still felt guilty about the fight, so he tried to be as good as he could for Miss Heath.

The semi-final was going to be played on Friday after school and Mr Giles had told everyone he would put the team up on the notice board on Wednesday afternoon. This meant Wednesday was the hardest day of all for William to focus. His concentration was so bad in Maths he had to ask Tom which page they should be on. Then a few minutes later, William had to ask which question they were on. Then only a few seconds later, he had to ask Tom how to answer the question.

"Is this how it's going to be when you're a famous rugby player?" Tom whispered back to him. "You'll just get us normal folk to do all your work for you? Look, it's easy, it's..."

"Tom! You've been talking to William all through this lesson. Stop asking him for help!"

"Sorry Miss Heath," said Tom.

"That's not good enough, Tom," said Miss Heath. "If you've got a question for William, then you can ask me. Up you get, what is it?"

Tom stood up at his desk.

"No, Miss Heath, it was just..." and he looked at William. William shook his head as if to say don't tell her.

"Just what, Tom?"

Tom winked and smiled at William and turned back to Miss Heath.

"It's just I was telling William this joke I heard on TV last night." And although Miss Heath tried to get Tom to be quiet and sit back down, he proceeded to tell the whole class a joke about ducks playing ice hockey with swans.

The joke wasn't actually very funny, but Tom told it with such enthusiasm even the girls at the front of the class, especially Abigail and Hayley, were almost crying with laughter and even Miss Heath was laughing by the end.

"Ok, Tom, sit down. And leave your joke telling to break time, please."

At lunch time, Tom had to repeat the whole incident to Finlay, which included telling the joke again. Finlay laughed almost as much as the girls had and William found himself chuckling again.

As they were all laughing, they saw Stephen and Harry approaching them. Stephen stepped ahead of Harry and joined in with the laughter.

"You're right," he said, still laughing. "It is funny that Tom's as ugly as that." The other three were quiet now. "And as for Finlay... Ow!"

Harry punched Stephen.

"Just leave them alone," he said. "They're ok." Then Harry turned to William, "Told you!"

"Told me what?"

"Have you not seen? Gilesy's put the team up."

William jumped up and ran off to look at the notice board and Tom and Finlay tried to follow after him. As they ran off, they could hear Stephen and Harry squabbling, and then Stephen said "Ow!" again as Harry punched him for a second time.

Tom and Finlay caught up with William at the notice board and as soon as he saw them his face broke out into the biggest grin.

"I'm in! I'm in!" he said.

"Knew you would be," said Tom, giving William a high five.

"Well done!" said Finlay, grinning.

"Maybe you won't be so annoying now and you might be able to concentrate on something for more than 30 seconds," said Tom.

"What?" said William. "Have I?" But Tom and Finlay just laughed and the three of them walked back to the playground.

On Friday, William's nerves were back at full strength, although this time it was the match itself he was nervous about. The match was away at the other school and so the rugby team were able to leave class 15 minutes before everyone else. As William stood up to leave, Miss Heath wished him luck in the game and then Tom started to clap. To William's embarrassment the whole class clapped and he couldn't leave the classroom quickly enough.

In the corridor, he saw a couple of the Year 6 boys and was a bit surprised when one of them said, "Oi, William!" and beckoned him to join their group as they walked to the minibus.

Many of the players were chatting and a few were even singing on the way to the match. There was even talk of who they thought they might play in the final, but Mr Giles soon told them to be quiet.

"Concentrate on this game first," he told them. "Let's win this game, then we can talk about the final on the way back."

The school they were playing against was called Welton and it was about a half hour drive away. Once they arrived, they got off the minibus and were met by the Welton teacher in charge of their rugby team. It seemed he and Mr Giles knew each other; they shook hands, shared a joke and chatted. The Northbrook team was directed to their changing room and they went to get ready for the match.

William knew he was going to be playing outside centre, so he got changed quietly and concentrated on what he had to do. He thought about the match and about making tackles. He thought about running hard and making passes. It was almost as if he was practising the game in his head before they actually played.

Just as William was starting to put his boots on, Mr Giles came in to give the team talk. But William couldn't listen to what he was saying because as he pulled his lace tight to tie up his boot, the lace snapped in his hand. William looked around the changing room in a panic. He wanted to ask if anyone had a spare lace, but they were all listening quietly to Mr Giles.

He realised even if he asked it was unlikely anyone would have one anyway. So William took the snapped lace out of his boot and re-laced it from halfway up the tongue. When he put it on again he knew it was still loose on his foot, even though it was tied as tight as possible.

William ran out with the rest of the team, but every step he took on his left foot he thought he felt his foot slip. Fortunately, the warm-up before the match helped to take his mind off his loose boot and before he knew it, William was lining up to start the match with everyone else.

This is it, William thought to himself. The cup semi-final and if we win this, we'll be in the final. He looked around him at his teammates and then the match was underway.

Northbrook kicked off; they chased the ball well and the forwards managed to turn the ball over in the ruck. The forwards tried to make more ground and there were a couple more runs and rucks before the scrum half passed it out to the backs and down the line. The Welton backs were still not fully ready after the kickoff - either that or they were expecting the forwards to keep the ball for a bit longer. Whatever the reason, they were caught out of position and Northbrook had an overlap. As the ball came to William, all he needed to do was pass it out once more to his winger and Northbrook would be free to score the first try, all within the first two minutes.

As the ball was passed to William, he caught it cleanly and took two steps forward before getting ready to pass. Just as he was about to release the ball, his left foot slipped inside his boot. William managed to keep his balance, but he stumbled and instead of passing the ball, his concentration was drawn to his boot. He glanced down at it and by the time he looked up again, the Welton team had reorganised and William was hit by an extremely hard tackle. William knocked the ball on and the opportunity was lost.

The winger sighed and glared at William and they could hear Mr Giles on the sideline trying to be positive.

"Let's try to be more clinical, boys, but well played," he shouted as he clapped.

As the scrum was taking place, William bent down to re-adjust his boot. But there was nothing he could really do, he'd just have to hope it didn't slip again.

Although Welton won the scrum, the Northbrook forwards managed to keep them pinned inside their own 22. For a few minutes the play was concentrated there. Welton just couldn't find a way past the Northbrook players to be able to advance up the pitch. The ball went from side to side with all the Northbrook players, William included, making some big tackles to keep Welton pinned in.

After a few minutes of good defending and tackling, the Northbrook players found themselves out of position and William had two attackers running at him. He prepared himself to tackle the player with the ball and hoped that he wouldn't be able to pass it to his teammate. As they came closer, William launched himself to his right to make the tackle. But just at that moment William's foot slipped again, his leg went from under him, and he fell forward. He was able to wrap his arms around the player's legs and make the tackle, but because he was falling, he had no power in it and the Welton player was able to run through it as if William had tried to stop him with a tissue.

Fortunately for Northbrook, their winger was able to catch the attacker and Welton couldn't reach the try line. Northbrook managed to collect the ball and kick it in to touch just over the halfway line.

William knew it was his fault again and the winger glared at him for a second time. William almost hoped the ball wouldn't come to him anymore as he didn't want to mess it up again.

From the line out, Welton took the ball back into their own half, but then kicked it long into the Northbrook half. The three fastest Welton players raced after the ball and there was only the Northbrook full back defending. William turned to sprint back as fast as he could but he just couldn't catch up at all. He couldn't understand it, it was as if he was running through treacle. William watched as the Welton players collected the ball and with a couple of passes they easily beat the Northbrook full back and scored the first try of the match.

As the Welton players were celebrating, William heard Mr Giles call his name and wave over to him. He turned to jog over to the sideline and looked down to realise he only had one boot on. His left boot was stuck in the pitch up near the hallway line. So, William hobbled up to collect it, before he went across to Mr Giles. "It looks like you're having some trouble with your boots, son. Why don't you have a little rest for a few minutes," Mr Giles said to him and signalled to Jasper to go on in William's place.

William threw his boot onto the floor and kicked it along the ground. 'Stupid, stupid boot! It's just not fair,' he thought to himself. He sat down on the grass and sulked.

The match carried on, but William wasn't watching it. He could hear Mr Giles shouting at the team and the other subs getting excited and he assumed it was going well for Northbrook, but he wasn't really sure. He didn't even bother to get up and join the team for the half-time team talk. 'What was the point?' he thought to himself.

In the end, Welton only managed to score one try, the one when William had lost his boot. Although they had come close a few other times they didn't manage any more, while Northbrook scored four and won the match 28-7. The Northbrook team was going to the final and on the pitch the players were all celebrating. Well, all except William who was still sitting on the sideline sulking. William was pretty sure even if his team was going to the final, he wouldn't be going as there was no way he'd be picked after how he had just played.

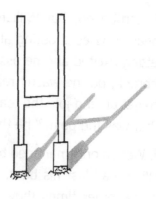

17

The half hour journey back to school seemed like the longest thirty minutes of William's life. William just sat quietly at the back of the minibus with his eyes closed, pretending to be asleep. Everyone else in the team was laughing, singing and remembering different parts of the match. William just wanted to forget it all. They were also discussing the final and which side they thought they would play. William didn't care because he knew he wouldn't be picked...

When they arrived back at school most of the team had parents there waiting for them and so they ran off the minibus to excitedly tell them what had happened. William was the last one to get off the bus and his mum had overheard all the other players, so when she saw him she excitedly threw her arms around him.

"Yay! You're in the final. Well done, superstar!"

William just shrugged, fought his way out of the embrace and started walking home. Confused, his mum followed him.

"What's up with you, misery guts?" she said when she caught up with him. "I thought you'd be pleased you won."

"*They* won," William corrected. "I didn't have anything to do with it. I was rubbish."

"I'm sure you weren't," his mum said, trying to console him.

"I was. My laces broke and I couldn't run and I got tackled and then he ran past me and my boot was in the mud and even Mr Giles thought I was rubbish."

William's mum couldn't really understand what William was saying as he'd started to cry by now and he refused to look at her, he'd said it all to the ground in front of his feet. She knew he was upset and tried to give him another hug, but William shrugged her off again and walked ahead quicker. He just wanted to get home and forget about the rugby match, in fact forget this whole day had even happened.

By the time they had arrived back at his mum's flat, William had stopped crying, but he certainly hadn't cheered up. He went straight to his room and lay down on the bed. His mum quietly knocked on the door, but William just ignored her. She knocked again and this time

William grunted. She knocked a third time, but didn't wait for an answer and walked straight in. She sat down on the bed next to William, who had rolled over so his back was towards her.

"So, it didn't go very well then," she said gently, trying to coax an answer out of William.

"NO!"

"I'm sure it can't have been that bad. I bet nobody else even noticed."

"Pfff," was all William could manage in response.

"Oh, come on, I bet you played better than you think."

William gave a big sigh, rolled over to face his mum and sat up a bit.

"I was awful. My laces broke, I couldn't run and Mr Giles subbed me after only about ten minutes. I won't get picked for the final and it doesn't matter because I hate rugby anyway." He fell back onto the bed and rolled over so his back was towards his mum again.

His mum wasn't sure how to respond.

"Oh," was all she could manage. "Do you want some tea? I can make you macaroni cheese if you like."

"I'm not hungry," said William and he lay on his bed determined to continue sulking.

His mum stood quietly for a minute or two. She took an intake of breath as if she was about to say something, but then changed her mind and slipped out of the room, leaving William to it. About 30 minutes later there was another knock at the door.

"I'm still not hungry," William said.

"Well, that's lucky," said his dad's voice, "cos I haven't got any food."

"Dad! What are you doing here?"

"Your mum called me, she was worried because you were so upset. Can I come in?"

William stayed with his back to the door,

"Suppose so."

"What's this all about? I thought your team won and you were in the final?"

William just shrugged. His dad had to persuade him to talk and finally he told his dad all about the match again. How his lace snapped, how he got tackled, how he lost his boot. how he couldn't run so they scored a try and how he was substituted.

"So, it doesn't even matter if we won, cos I won't be picked for the final anyway!" was how William finished his story and then he rolled back over and turned to face away from his dad.

His dad ruffled his hair.

"I think you're probably wrong, but I understand how you feel. I'll leave you to sulk for a bit," he said as he got up and left the room.

About five minutes later his dad knocked on the door again and walked straight in without waiting for a response. In his hand he held William's left boot, but now it was fully laced up.

"Your mum had some spare laces and so I threw out the snapped one," he said. "Come on, we're going out to the park to see if it still fits ok."

"Urghh!'" William just groaned and stayed where he was.

"Come on, William, now. Let's go."

"But, Dad..."

"No buts, let's go!"

William sighed and reluctantly got up off the bed.

They walked down to the park without saying a word to each other. When they got to the park William sat down on the bench and his dad spent a long time carefully putting William's boots on for him. He made William stand up and he tested how much room his feet had and whether his toes were at the end of the boot. Then he untied them and tied them up again and did the same test all over again. This went on about four times before he was happy with the boots. Once he was, he told William to walk to the edge of the football pitch and turn round and come back again.

"How do they feel?"

"Yeah, they're ok."

"Great, now run over to the goalpost and back again." William set off jogging to the goalpost.

"Come on, sprint. Really test them out," his dad shouted as William turned round to set off back again.

William sprinted hard and the boots felt good. Now they were secure with the new laces he felt like he could run really fast. Just as he was about to reach his dad again, a rugby ball came flying towards him. William hadn't even seen his dad carrying the ball, but now he was passing it to him.

William caught the ball and was about to pass it back, but his dad had moved. "Over here," he shouted. William turned to his left and passed it back to his dad. His dad caught it and returned it to William in one move, but the ball was a little bit in front of him and he had to take a couple of steps forward and reach out for it. By the time he had caught the ball, his dad had moved again, so William had to spin round to pass it back to him.

They kept this up for about ten minutes, constantly passing and moving with the ball flying between them. Suddenly, after receiving one pass, William's dad gently kicked the ball back to William. The ball went much higher and William had to take a few steps backwards to be in the right position to catch it, but he did catch it and then he tried to kick it back to his dad.

William's kick was a bit wobbly, but his dad managed to catch it and so the next ten minutes were spent kicking the ball to each other.

After several kicks each, and without any warning, William's dad did a very hard, high and long kick. William had to turn round and sprint after the ball. He had no way of catching it, but he managed to pick it up after the third bounce. The ball had been kicked so far it took William four kicks to get it all the way back to his dad.

Instead of kicking the ball again, William's dad picked it up and said,

"I'm exhausted, kiddo. Let's go back and see how your mum is getting on."

William was surprised by how much he was enjoying it.

"Can't we just have five more minutes?" he asked.

"I tell you what, let's do a few gentle passes to each other as we're walking back," his dad said. "But first let's take those boots off and put your shoes back on."

They walked all the way back to William's mum's flat with the rugby ball flying between them. They had to be careful to dodge an old lady walking her dog and William dropped the ball as they were going round a corner. It bounced into the road in front of a car and William's dad retrieved the ball from the road and waved an apology to the driver.

As they got back, William's mum said,

"There you are, perfect timing. William, you need a good wash and please change your t-shirt and put a clean jumper on as well."

"Actually, Fiona, I wouldn't mind a quick wash as well, if that's ok," said William's dad.

"Of course, Mark. Help yourself to one of the fresh towels on the shelf. Why don't you go first and William can tell me how it was at the park?"

A few minutes later William's dad came out of the bathroom, buttoning up his shirt. His hair was damp and brushed neatly and his face looked a bit pink.

"Your turn, William," he said.

When William came out of his bedroom after getting washed and changed, his mum and dad were standing close together in the kitchen. There was a bottle of wine open between them and they each had a glass in their hands and there were some takeaway cartons on the work surface.

William waited and watched for a minute. He wasn't sure what it was. Then he realised. They looked happy! He couldn't actually remember the last time he had seen them like this. William's dad told a joke and William's mum tapped his hand as she started to laugh. She threw her head back as she laughed and saw William out of the corner of her eye.

"Hey," she said. "All clean? I hope you don't mind, but I thought the three of us would have a Chinese for dinner."

"Of course, I don't mind," said William. "I'll set the table."

William had his usual Chinese dish of chicken and cashew nuts with fried rice and he had loads of prawn crackers too. The happy mood and laughing continued around the table as they were eating. William's mum had cleared all her work things away and they sat and ate and talked and laughed.

When they had finished, William's mum said,

"I think I've got some ice cream in the freezer. Why don't you two sit on the sofa and we can have ice cream in front of the TV?"

William and his dad sat down and put the TV on.

"Right," said his dad, "What's on tonight?" He started to flick through the guide on the TV. "What about this film?" he asked.

"Yeah, I'm pretty sure I've heard the kids at school saying it's good," said William.

William had actually never heard of the film, all he knew was that it started in ten minutes and wouldn't finish for over two hours. If it was a good film then it would mean the three of them would stay like this for at least another two hours.

"Ok," said his dad. "Let's give it a go."

As William's mum came back with the ice cream, William's dad looked up at her and said,

"William's chosen this film for us to watch. Ok?"

"I don't see why not. Here's your ice cream. Enjoy!"

"Do you want to sit here, Mum?" said William starting to stand up from the sofa. "I'll sit on the chair."

"It's ok," said his mum. "You stay where you are," and she sat down in the chair instead.

The ice cream was vanilla flavoured, but with swirls of something which could have been toffee and little pieces of chocolate brownie in it. It was lovely and the three of them ate in silence as the news and weather finished before the film started.

The film was ok, but certainly not what William was expecting from the title. At least there weren't any awkward kissy bits (which made him squirm) or any swearing which might have made his parents might turn it off.

"Are you sure this is what you wanted to watch?" asked his dad after about 20 minutes.

"Yeah, yeah. I think it's meant to get better later on," said William. But he wasn't bothered whether it got any better or not, he was just enjoying sitting there.

A few minutes later his mum cleared the ice cream bowls away and she came back with two glasses of wine.

"I thought I might as well open another bottle," she said and smiled as she handed William's dad one of the glasses.

"Yeah, that's great. Thanks, Fiona," he said. He smiled back to her as he took the glass. William just smiled to himself.

In the end, the film didn't get any better and William fell asleep on the sofa before it finished. When he woke up, his dad was standing by the front door, putting his jacket on.

"Thanks for inviting me over, Fiona," he said to her with a smile. "It was great to spend some time together."

"I'm glad you came," she replied. She was smiling as well. "He'll always need his dad and you're really good for him."

"Well, you seem to be doing a really good job of everything, of all... this." William's dad had waved his hand around the flat when he said that last word. "Anyway, let me say goodbye to sleeping beauty over there."

He walked over to William,

"Oh, you're awake! The film was weird, you probably did the right thing by falling asleep," he said. "Have a good weekend and I'll see you after school on Monday." He ruffled William's hair, then gave him a hug.

"Thanks again, Fiona," he said as got to the front door.

"You're welcome," she said and they hugged. They both laughed slightly as the hug broke and then looked at each other and laughed again. They stayed looking at each other until William's dad finally stepped outside of the flat.

"Goodnight Mark," William's mum said as she waved goodbye to him.

Once she closed the door, she turned back to William.

"Come on, you. Time to fall asleep in your bed, not on the sofa. Off you go."

William fell asleep within just a few minutes of getting into bed, with a huge grin on his face.

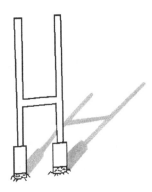

18

Tom and Finlay were a bit nervous around William at school on Monday morning. They were worried he'd still be in a terrible mood after the rugby. They had heard about the semi-final and what had happened to William, so they were very surprised when he was happy and smiling all morning. Even being asked to read aloud in English class hadn't knocked William out of his good mood.

At break they all sat together and Tom just decided to come out with it.

"How come you're so smiley? We thought you'd be a right misery guts cos the rugby was so rubbish."

"Tom!" said Finlay staring at him.

"What? You'd said he'd be a misery too."

William laughed.

"Yeah, the rugby was rubbish, but it's only rugby, isn't it? And I'm gonna thrash you at Top Trumps anyway."

Finlay just looked at Tom and shrugged. This was very odd for William, but they were pleased he wasn't being miserable, so the three of them played cards together.

William's good mood stayed for the next couple of days and nothing seemed to shift the smile from his face. When he went round to his mum's flat after school on Wednesday, he hugged her as soon as she let him in.

"Wow, ok!" she said, "What's that for?"

"Just because," he said and went into his bedroom to get changed.

When she came in later to ask him about tea, he asked, "Is there any more of the swirly toffee ice cream?"

"I think so."

"Can I have some of it for pudding?"

"Sure, if you like. You'll probably finish it off, then."

"Will you buy some more?"

"I suppose so."

"That's good. Dad really liked it too didn't he, when he was here?"

William's mum laughed, "Yeah, I suppose he did. Anyway, tea will be ready soon," she said as she left his room.

They had a lovely evening together, including the swirly toffee ice cream for pudding, and William was still smiling at school on Thursday morning. Tom was off school for the morning as he had a dentist's appointment, so when it came to break time, it was just William and Finlay. It was strange, but without Tom everything just seemed quieter.

Finlay sat down on the bench at break time and got the Top Trumps cards out ready to play with William. He shuffled the cards, but before he started dealing he turned to William, "How is everything, you know, with your mum and dad?"

"I think it's gonna be ok!" said William with a massive grin.

"Oh, that's good. I found it really hard at first when my dad left, but you get used to it. I mean things are different for you, cos you still see your dad. I'm not even sure where my dad lives."

"No, I don't think I'll have to get used to it," said William. "I'm pretty sure my mum and dad are gonna get back together."

And then William told Finlay all about Friday night and how his parents had laughed and drank wine together.

"I don't think I've seen them laugh like that for ages. They're def gonna get back together."

"That's great," smiled Finlay. "But it doesn't always happen like that you know. My mum tried to stay friends with my dad at first, but now she won't even say his name and just calls him 'the idiot'."

"Yeah, but my parents are different," said William. "For a start, my dad's not an idiot!"

225

Finlay laughed.

"My dad's ok too," he said. "At least I think he is. I don't see him much. But I'm just saying, don't get too excited."

"No!" said William. "I'm gonna get excited and it's all gonna be ok. You just watch." And with that the bell rang and they went back into their classrooms.

That weekend, William was with his dad and they had their usual Chinese takeaway on Friday night.

"Shall we invite Mum round to have a takeaway with us tonight?" asked William.

"Ha! No, I'm sure she's busy."

"She might not be. I bet she'd love to come round. You could phone her."

"Let's leave it as just the two of us tonight."

"But it was good last Friday all three of us having a Chinese together, wasn't it, Dad?"

"Yeah, it was nice," said his dad, smiling.

William smiled too. He didn't ask again to invite his mum, but he did continue to smile throughout their meal. His dad opened a bottle of wine when they'd finished eating and William looked at him warily.

"Just a couple of glasses, I promise."

William's hand subconsciously moved to where his dad had scratched him the other weekend.

"Yeah, ok," he mumbled, but the smile had left his face.

226

"I promise," his dad repeated. "Listen, why don't we watch a film together and you can help yourself some ice cream?"

So, William went to the freezer to get himself some ice cream while his dad went to choose a film to watch. He reached in for the raspberry ice cream he'd had before, but next to it was a new, unopened tub of the same vanilla, toffee and chocolate brownie ice cream his mum had served last weekend. William was smiling again.

"I think there's some already open, use that first," his dad shouted, so although he was very tempted to open the toffee one, William took a big bowlful of the raspberry ice cream through and sat down in front of the TV with his dad.

William did some science and geography homework on Saturday, while his dad tidied the garden. On Sunday morning, they went for a long walk and took the rugby ball with them, so they could pass it between themselves on the quiet back streets. When they got to the park, they passed it around a bit more and spent nearly an hour running around together, until William's dad had to stop for a rest.

"Don't forget I'm an old man," he said laughing as he sat down. "I don't have your energy."

William laughed at him and ran round the park again, just to show how much energy he had left.

As they were walking to school together on Monday morning, William said to his dad,

"It's a shame Mum has to live in the flat all on her own, isn't it?"

"I suppose so, but she's not on her own all the time. You're there sometimes."

"Yeah, but I mean without you," said William.

"That's just the way it is though, kiddo."

"But it would be nicer if she came back home with us, wouldn't it?"

"Well... I mean... Oh look, there's Tom waiting for you," said his dad, pointing at Tom who was standing in his usual spot.

As William walked up to meet Tom, Finlay joined them both from his house and they set off across the field to school. William turned round to wave to his dad and then nudged Finlay.

"It's definitely gonna happen," he whispered grinning. "It might even happen this weekend."

"You're playing rugby this weekend, aren't you?"

"Oh, I won't be picked," said William grinning and shrugging at the same time.

"What are you two muttering about?" asked Tom.

"William thinks he won't be picked for the rugby final," said Finlay.

"Don't be daft!" said Tom. "You're one of the best players." Then Tom dodged and weaved his way through some imaginary opponents across the field. Finlay and William laughed and followed him towards school.

At break and lunchtime, William wanted to talk about his parents again with Finlay, but Tom was always around and for some reason he didn't want to talk to Tom about it. Finlay understood him. Finlay had been through it and Finlay was someone you could sit and have a quiet conversation with. Tom, as nice as he was, wasn't someone like that. They did manage to talk a little bit whenever Tom ran off to chase someone across the playground.

"Don't get your hopes up, adults are weird," was all Finlay could say whenever William did mention it. But William just grinned back at him.

"Def gonna happen," was William's only reply.

At the end of lunchtime, Harry came up to the three of them in the playground. Tom and Finlay both went silent and looked nervous as he arrived, but William looked up and smiled.

"Alright, Harry?" he said.

"Ready for Saturday then?" said Harry.

"Eh?"

"The rugby, you idiot!"

"Oh, I won't be playing," said William. "You saw what happened in the semi-final."

"Don't be daft! You're picked. You're a sub."

"What?" William spluttered. "Really? Really?"

"Are you calling me a liar?" said Harry menacingly. Tom and Finlay slunk back further and tried to be even quieter.

Then Harry burst out laughing. "Of course you're picked. You're a great player, you just had one bad match." Then he strolled off. William sat there shocked.

"Told you," said Tom. "Come on, let's go and check the board."

But before they had even left the bench, the bell rang and they had to go back into class.

William spent most of the afternoon in a bit of a daze. He had been certain he wasn't going to get picked. He was also certain something was going to happen with his parents this weekend, but how could it, if he was playing rugby? Or maybe it could happen while he was playing rugby. Actually, would he even play? He was only picked as sub and he had been rubbish in the semi-final, he probably wouldn't even get on the pitch. In which case, should he cancel and tell Mr Giles he couldn't play? That way he could help out with his parents.

All these thoughts whirled round William's brain while he was supposed to be concentrating on lessons.

As soon as the final lesson ended, Tom and William made their way to the noticeboard to see the team. Finlay was already waiting for them both there. Finlay was nodding and grinning and as William saw the teamsheet, he could see his name listed as one of the subs.

Tom slapped him on the back and Finlay just grinned at him.

"Well, that's my Saturday morning sorted," said Tom. "Eh?"

"We're coming to watch you play," said Finlay.

"We're coming to watch you win!" said Tom, grinning.

The final was going to be played at the ground of the local professional rugby team and in the school assembly last week the headmaster had suggested to the whole school they could come and support the team.

William was even more confused now. And what was the funny feeling in his stomach? Was it nerves already?

As the three of them walked home across the field William was quiet, but as usual Tom was chatty enough for all them. He was telling William how brilliant he was going to be and explaining, in quite a lot of detail - much of it completely inaccurate - about how they were going to win and score lots of 'goals' as Tom called them by mistake.

As they reached the corner of the field and saw William's dad waiting, Tom shouted out, "See you at the final on Saturday, Mr Brown!"

"See you there, Tom," said William's dad. "But I might see you here a few more times before then."

"Oh yeah, I forgot about that," said Tom and he set off walking home whistling and singing to himself.

William waved goodbye to Finlay and went over to his smiling dad.

"So you have been picked then," he said.

"Well, only as a sub."

"That's still great news," said his dad and they talked about rugby all the way home.

William sat in front of the TV and watched his cartoons as usual, but the conversation was all about rugby again while they ate. It seemed as if his dad was more excited about the final than William.

"Do you know what time kick-off is?"

"And what time do you need to be there to get ready and warm-up?"

"I know where the ground is, but I don't know how much parking there will be there. Do you know if the players can definitely park there, or should I check out nearby car parks?"

"Is there a presentation ceremony after the match?"

Of course, William didn't know the answer to any of the questions, but it didn't stop his dad asking even more. Finally, when William could get a word in, he asked a question of his own, "What about Mum?"

"What about her?"

"Well...." William wasn't sure what he wanted to say about all the weekend plans he thought might be happening. "I mean... will she be coming to watch?"

"I expect so, but you'll have to ask her. Actually, you'll be there this weekend anyway won't you? So, she'll be taking you to the match."

"Will you watch the match with her?" asked William hopefully.

"I'm sure there'll be lots of fans there. I might not be able to find her even if I wanted to," his dad replied as he stood up to clear away the plates.

William decided he would talk to his mum about everything - the rugby, but especially when she might be moving back in with them - as soon as he could, but when he went round to her flat after school on Wednesday, she was too busy with work to talk. William was allowed to sit and watch television all afternoon as his mum had cleared away all her work stuff into her bedroom and she was working from there.

She would pop out to see if William was ok every now and again, but she was often on the phone at the same time. She would wave at him and stick her thumb up with a questioning face. William would reply by putting his thumb up and nodding. Then his mum would point to her phone and roll her eyes and mouth the word 'Sorry'. William would just put his thumb up again, smile and carry on watching TV.

Much later, his mum nipped out, switched the oven on and took something out of the freezer and put it into the warming oven. Then, about thirty minutes later, she came out of her room again, took it out of the oven and called William into the kitchen.

As she dished the food up, William's mum was talking about reports and accounts and clients and how important this was and a possible promotion and some of her colleagues, whose names William didn't catch. Actually, he only understood about half of what his mum was saying to him. She looked busy and tired and he was a bit worried about her, but she also seemed full of enthusiasm and passion and he liked that about her. In fact, she looked more determined and more contented than he'd seen her ever looking.

He had wanted to talk to her tonight, but he could see she was too busy, so William decided to wait until the weekend to discuss when she would be moving back home. Maybe they would watch the rugby match together and then all three of them could talk then.

William ate his lasagne in front of the TV and his mum went back into her room with hers.

When it was bedtime, his mum was very apologetic about all the time she had spent working.

"I'm so sorry, sweetheart," she said and then she started talking about reports and business things again.

"Mum... do you still like Dad?" William asked, out of the blue.

His mum stopped talking about work and looked at him.

"What do you mean?"

"You remember Dad. He's that funny looking bloke I spend time with sometimes."

His mum laughed.

"Of course I remember him, silly. And of course I still like him. I like that we've got you. I like that he's a good dad. And I like the fact we'll always be your mum and dad. Now, go to sleep." She kissed him on the forehead and stood up to walk out the room.

"OK, Mum. Don't work too hard," said William as he pulled the duvet up over his shoulders.

"Thank you, sweetheart. Sleep well," said William's mum as she turned off his bedroom light.

William smiled to himself. She had said she still liked him. Here was the proof he needed. They were definitely getting back together. He fell asleep almost instantly, with a big grin on his face.

When William woke up in the morning, his mum was already up and dressed in business clothes.

"Right, then. I've got a meeting this morning, so I'm going to drive you to school and then set off straight away from there. Get yourself ready and I'll drop you at school a bit early."

William poured himself a bowl of Cheerios and started eating.

"I've sent Sharon a message as well, so the boys know not to wait for you."

With a mouthful of Cheerios William looked up at his mum. 'Oog,' was all he could manage to say, but he was trying to ask who Sharon was.

Fortunately, his mum understood him, even through the Cheerios.

"Finlay's mum."

"Oh, yeah. Ok."

Then his mum chatted about how this could be a really important meeting and how she was excited, but nervous at the same time. She said something about promotion as well, but William couldn't follow it. Instead, he smiled and nodded while he wolfed down his breakfast. Once he had finished, he jumped up to get himself ready.

Because they were so early, there was hardly any traffic and it took them less than five minutes to drive round the corner to school.

"Good luck with your meeting," William said as he got out of the car.

"Thank you, sweetheart. Have a good day at school and I'll see you on Friday. I'll have more time then, so we can talk more then, I promise," his mum said.

William shut the car door and waved to his mum and she drove off in a hurry. He realised he was probably the first pupil to arrive at school that morning. Instead of waiting in an empty playground, he decided to walk over the field as if he was walking home from school and waited where he usually met up with Tom and Finlay.

He'd been there on his own for a couple of minutes when Finlay came out of his house.

"I thought you weren't coming this morning. My mum got a message from your mum."

"Yeah, but I was bored waiting at school on my own," said William.

"How was it at your mum's last night?"

"She was super busy with work, so I just watched TV.

Did you watch that programme about the old-fashioned TV programmes? The clothes they were wearing were hilarious!"

Finlay laughed.

"I bet they were. My mum has shown me some photos of when she was a kid. Her clothes are really funny."

"Yeah, I know. And my mum said they didn't even have phones back then to be able to take photos with!"

"Morning, you two," shouted Tom as he came round the corner. "You're here early, what are you talking about?"

"About how old Finlay's mum is," said William, laughing.

"And your parents," said Finlay. "In fact, all of our parents are ancient."

Tom started to tell a story about when his dad was at school and Finlay whispered to William,

"I meant to ask about, you know, any updates?"

"Not really. But my mum did say how much she still likes my dad," whispered William back to him, grinning from ear to ear.

Tom's story finished with his dad drinking milk in a classroom on his own and then throwing up on the floor. Tom clearly thought it was hilarious, but William and Finlay just shrugged and carried on walking.

The next couple of days passed by in a bit of a blur for William. He was still confused about his parents' situation and couldn't help thinking about it, but whenever he managed to push the issue out of his mind, the rugby popped in and he started thinking about that instead.

He still wasn't sure why he had been picked after he'd messed up so badly in the semi-final. And this was the final. With all those people watching. So maybe it was better that he was only a substitute, because if he didn't even get on to the pitch then he wouldn't be able to ruin everything again.

Sometimes for William, it was a relief just to try and concentrate on what the teacher was saying and to try and answer the questions during the lesson.

After school on Friday, he went round to his mum's. When he walked into the flat, she wasn't working and she certainly wasn't dressed as smartly as she been for her meeting on Thursday morning.

"This is... erm... different," said William when he saw his mum sitting on the sofa.

"Yeah. I've had the day off today. The meeting went so well yesterday my boss gave me the day off. Which was lucky really as Dominic and I went out for lunch and drinks after the meeting. In the end, we stayed out all afternoon and into the evening."

"Oh great, yeah. Wait a minute! Who's Dominic?"

His mum blushed slightly.

"Well, he's someone I work with and..."

"Oh, ok," said William and put the TV on.

"Can I watch a bit of TV with you?" his mum asked William.

"Of course, you can."

238

"Great. Then I'll cook some pasta for tea tonight and we can have a Chinese after the rugby tomorrow, if that's ok?"

William just nodded and carried on watching. When he turned round to his mum to explain what the aliens were doing at the school, her eyes were already closed and her head had dropped back onto the cushion.

William decided to let her sleep for a while. It was a double bill of the alien programme this week and then there were some cartoons on afterwards. But when one of the cartoon characters fell off a cliff and hit the ground with a big cartoon 'Bang!' it startled William's mum and she woke up.

"Oh, have I been asleep?" she asked, wiping a bit of dribble off her chin.

"Yeah."

"Oh, sorry. Was I snoring?"

"Not much," said William grinning.

"Oh, no," said his mum, sheepishly grinning back at him. "I'll just have to make a super delicious tea to make up for it." And she got up off the sofa and went into the kitchen, leaving William watching TV.

"This is really yummy," said William as he dug into the bowl of pasta.

"Oh, good. Am I forgiven for snoring then?"

"Of course, you are."

"Good. Let's talk about the rugby tomorrow. Kick-off is at 11 o'clock, but you must arrive by 10 o'clock to get changed and warm-up and all that stuff. So it means we'll have to leave here by 9:30 at the latest. Is your bag all ready?" William nodded. "You sure? Boots and mouth guard thing and socks? Will you need a towel so you can shower afterwards?"

"Oh, yeah. Suppose so."

"Ok. I'll get one out and put it on your bed after tea. I don't know what's going to happen straight after the match or when we might get home, so I've got some cereal bars for you in case you get hungry."

"Thanks, Mum."

"And, well... I've got a question to ask you."

"What is it?" asked William, with his mouth full of pasta.

"You know how I mentioned Dominic from work earlier?" William nodded. "Well, he is... or he might be... well at least he could be a bit more than a friend from work."

"You mean like a boss or something?" said William.

"No, not really. I mean more than a friend, more like a... well... like a boyfriend."

"Whose?"

"Mine, silly. I'm not too old to have a boyfriend you know," said William's mum.

William didn't know what to say. How could his mum have a boyfriend? What about his dad? What about them getting back together?

"Anyway, I wanted to ask if you'd mind if he came along to watch you play rugby tomorrow?"

William just nodded. He was afraid to say anything in case he started to cry. "Thank you, sweetheart," said William's mum. She gave him a kiss on the forehead and picked her plate up and took it to the sink.

All of a sudden, William wasn't hungry anymore. Tears filled his eyes and he could no longer see the last few pieces of pasta in his bowl. His insides felt like they were twisted in knots and his throat felt tight. He sat quietly, trying not to cry, while his mum tidied up in the kitchen.

"Actually, Mum, I'm really tired and I need a good night's sleep before the match tomorrow. So, I'm going to go to bed."

"This early, are you sure?"

William nodded. His mum gave him a hug and it took all of William's strength not to burst into tears in her arms, but as soon as he got into bed the tears came. He pulled the pillow over his face so his mum wouldn't hear him, but he cried and cried until he fell asleep.

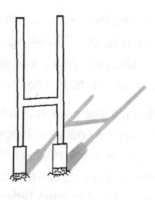

19

William woke up feeling exhausted. He hadn't slept well at all. He felt like he had no energy and the last thing he wanted to do today was play rugby. It's alright, he thought to himself, I'm only a sub anyway. I probably won't even get on the pitch.

He gave a big sigh and dragged himself out of bed. The first thing he did was to check his bag again. His mum had put the towel and a couple of cereal bars on the floor next to his bed, so he packed them in with the rest of his kit.

As he was mindlessly eating his cereal, his mum came out of her bedroom in her dressing gown.

"Did you sleep well? Are you all ready for the match?"

William just nodded. He wasn't ready at all, but how could he tell her? "I spoke to Dominic last night and he's looking to forward to watching the match - and to meeting you, of course."

William smiled, but the smile was only with his mouth. He definitely didn't smile with his eyes and he definitely wasn't smiling inside. He didn't know who this Dominic was, but he already didn't like him.

His mum hadn't noticed though, as she was busy getting herself some breakfast.

"Are you done in the bathroom?" she asked. "I still need a shower and then I need to get my hair ready. I don't want to look like I've spent too much time on it, but it's important I get it right. What should it look like for watching a rugby match do you think?" William just shrugged.

"No, of course you don't know. Silly question. Sorry. But what should I wear? I've got those nice, new jeans, but are they a bit too nice. What if I get them dirty? What do other mums wear?" William just looked at her this time.

"No, no. You're right. Okay. Anyway, I'm going into the bathroom. Make sure you're ready for 9:30." And off she went.

William went to his room to lie on his bed while he waited. He didn't even want to turn the TV on. His mum's bedroom door was open as he walked passed, she had five different jumpers laid out on her bed. William didn't understand what was going on, so he just shrugged again.

At about twenty past nine William's mum knocked on his bedroom door.

"Ok then, rugby superstar. Let's go!" she said.

William got off his bed, picked up his bag and opened his bedroom door. In front of him stood his mum, who was wearing a completely different jumper, which hadn't even been one of the ones on her bed earlier.

"Nice jumper," he said.

"Do you think so? Thank you."

"Didn't Dad buy it for you?"

"No, I don't think so," she paused. "Oh, maybe he did... actually, will it be warm enough for the rugby? I'll just quickly change it." And she went into her room.

She came out just a few seconds later wearing yet another jumper and said to William,

"Right, then. We're off to the final!"

They had to drive out of Northbrook and about ten miles to the town of Stanford. The rugby club was on the edge of the town, near the river. Stanford had been a good rugby team and in the top division years ago. They now played in a slightly lower league, but the ground was still bigger and better than anything William had ever seen before.

They had their own car park at the ground and William and his mum were able to drive through the gate marked, 'Players Only'. Once they'd parked, they saw a door which said 'Players' Entrance'. William opened the door and carefully looked inside. His mum waved at him to carry on and then blew him a kiss.

"William! Good lad!" It was Mr Giles' voice. "In you come. We're in changing room four. Most of the lads are already here. Before you go, I just want to say, you're sub today, but you'll almost certainly get on the pitch. So, be ready to give your all and to play as well as I know you can. Off you go."

William walked down the corridor, found the changing room and went in to get changed.

When all the players were changed, they went outside to warm-up. They'd never done this before a match, but Mr Giles had said it was important and something about atmosphere. William hadn't been listening properly, he didn't want to be there and despite what Mr Giles had said he was convinced he wasn't going to be playing anyway.

When they ran outside, the first thing William did was look around for his parents and to see if he could see Dominic.

The ground had one big stand, which although it was called a 'stand', was where everyone sat down to watch the match. The stand ran almost the whole length of the pitch along one side and had at least thirty rows of seats. The other three sides of the pitch had no seating at all, but had a railing around it which people could lean against to watch the match.

He could see his mum near the back of the stand. She was on her own. Good, thought William. Then he heard his name shouted out. Just in front of his mum were Tom and Finlay, sitting with Finlay's mum. As soon as they'd seen William, both the boys jumped up and started shouting.

William gave them all a shy wave and joined the rest of the team.

The Northbrook team all did some stretching, then after a few minutes they started to run around and pass the ball to each other.

As they were doing that, the other team came out of the changing rooms. At first William assumed there had been a mistake and that this was an adult team. Then he heard the whispers from his teammates.

"Oh no! It's Mickleborough."

"They look even bigger! How is that possible?"

"I'm sure that one's got a beard."

When they were back in the changing room, Mr Giles called the team together.

"We nearly beat them last time and we've got better and better every match we've played. You can see they're big lads, but you've all got the skill to beat them. You'll have to play well, you'll have to tackle hard, but I know you can do it."

Mr Giles then called out the team again and gave everyone their match shirts. William had Number 18 and was one of the seven substitutes.

"I'll try to give you all a game if I can," Mr Giles said to the seven of them.

By the time the team ran back out onto the pitch, even more people had turned up to watch. The stand had lots of different groups of parents, brothers, sisters, grandmas and grandads and, as William knew, friends. The groups sat together in twos, threes and fours. Sometimes those groups had joined up and there was a bigger group of about ten, but between each of the groups was a gap of few seats in all directions. This meant the stand looked almost full and already there was a lot of noise coming from it.

William looked up and Tom and Finlay waved enthusiastically. William's mum was still on her own, but she was talking to Finlay's mum who was two rows in front of her.

On the opposite edge of the pitch, the railing was almost full of people standing to watch the match. William looked along and there, almost level with the half-way line, was his dad. William waved and his dad put his thumbs up.

The team did a few final warm-ups and then it was time for kick-off. William and the other substitutes had to leave the pitch, but they were able to sit down in the dugout to watch the match.

As he left the pitch, William glanced up again. Tom and Finlay were still being enthusiastic and they waved at

William. William was about to wave back when he saw someone walking along the row behind them.

The late arriving spectator excused himself, as he disturbed some of the people who were already sitting down, before he stood next to William's mum. He opened his arms wide and shrugged at the same time as if to apologise, but William's mum just smiled and waved it off. Then he sat down next to William's mum and gave her a kiss. A proper kiss on the lips.

William stopped walking and stared up at the stand. One of the other substitutes had to nudge him to keep him moving. When they got to the dugout William just slumped into the seat.

The other substitutes were excitedly chatting about the match, about who was here to support them and about how big the Mickleborough players were, but William wasn't listening. William was concentrating on what he had seen. He was trying to remember exactly what Dominic looked like so he could hate him even more.

William was so lost in his thoughts he didn't even notice Northbrook had scored the first try of the match within a few minutes of the kick-off. He looked up when he heard the excitement of Mr Giles and the other substitutes.

He was still lost in his thoughts, when a few minutes later there was more excitement in the dugout. He looked up again expecting another try, but instead all the players were crowded round someone lying on the floor near the far touchline. Mr Giles ran out and over his shoulder shouted at the substitutes to warm-up. The other substitutes jumped up and started jogging up and down. William stayed in his seat for a few seconds, but reluctantly joined them.

A few minutes later, Mr Giles came back to the dugout with his arm around Simon, the winger, who was holding his ribs. Simon grimaced as he sat down and Mr Giles looked at William.

"Right, you're on!"

"Me?"

"Of course you! Jasper has moved out to the wing and you're outside centre."

"Yeah, yeah. Right."

William threw his tracksuit top off and fiddled with his shirt. Mr Giles had to give him a nudge, "Go on then, lad!" before William took a deep breath and ran onto the pitch.

Even in all the noise of the ground he could hear Tom and Finlay excitedly cheering. Despite his mood, it made William smile. He looked up to them.

Behind Tom and Finlay, he saw his mum wave to him. He was just about to wave back when he saw Dominic wave as well. William stopped smiling and ran out to join his teammates.

He'd only been on the pitch a few minutes when Mickleborough had a scrum. They played the ball out of the back of the scrum and started to pass it along the line. William could see Mickleborough's outside centre and he had a clear route to tackle him. William prepared himself, crouched low and thought about Dominic sitting next to his mum. He launched himself at his opposite number and even though he was a couple of inches taller than William, he tackled him hard.

The tackle took the Mickleborough centre back a few paces and then straight down onto the grass. William stood up, triumphantly.

Then he heard the whistle blow for a penalty for a late tackle. The centre had passed the ball out to the winger just before William had tackled him and so William's great tackle counted for nothing.

William looked up and saw his dad on the touchline. His dad just shrugged his shoulders and waved William to keep on going.

But William just couldn't get into the game, everything he did he seemed to be a couple of seconds behind his teammates. Twice William was tackled in a promising attacking position for Northbrook when he should have passed the ball out to the winger sooner.

The rest of the Northbrook team were playing well though. The forwards were working hard against the bigger Mickleborough players and weren't being pushed around. Harry almost managed a break of his own out of the back of a ruck, but he was tackled a few metres from the line.

Eventually though, the Mickleborough pressure told and their forwards moved the ball down the pitch with ruck after ruck until they reached the Northbrook try line and scored the try. The angle was difficult for the kicker, and he missed the conversion, which meant Northbrook's lead had been cut to 7-5.

"Keep going, lads! Keep it tight!" Mr Giles shouted at the team.

But William still couldn't quite concentrate on the match. If his mum was with Dominic, did it mean she'd never move back in with William and his dad?

He was busy thinking about this when the Mickleborough centre ran past him with the ball in his hand. William realised what was happening too late and although he tried to make a tackle he was in the wrong the position and the Mickleborough player was able to break through easily.

Alex stepped inside from the wing to cover for William, but the Mickleborough centre passed the ball out to his now unmarked winger who ran down the wing to score in the corner. The Mickleborough kicker couldn't make this conversion either, but now Mickleborough were 10-7 in the lead.

The game stayed tight for the next few minutes, then just before the end of the half, Northbrook had a break. The ball was fed out to William, who had Alex outside him on the wing. They only had the Mickleborough full back to beat and William was trying to decide whether to pass out to Alex or to try and beat the full back himself when he was tackled hard from the side. The Mickleborough centre had recovered his position, but William hadn't even seen him.

The ball spilled forward from the tackle and William was waiting for the referee to blow the whistle for a scrum, but he played the advantage instead. The delay from William meant that the full back was able to pick up the ball and run up the pitch. With support from his winger he was able to beat Alex and the Northbrook full back and score an easy try under the posts. This time the Mickleborough kicker had no problem with the conversion and Mickleborough were ahead 17-7.

William knew the try was his fault. He knew he was playing badly, but he just couldn't seem to concentrate on the game. He didn't want to look over to Tom and Finlay as he was almost embarrassed they were here to cheer him on while he was playing so badly. And he certainly didn't want to see his mum sitting next to Dominic.

He looked the other way to try and spot his dad and get some support from him, but he couldn't see him anywhere along the railing. He wasn't where he had been standing near the halfway line and he couldn't see him anywhere else.

He's gone home, thought William. He can see how rubbish I am and he doesn't want to watch anymore. William felt even worse now. He felt like he'd been winded. He had what felt like a big hole in his stomach and his arms and legs just felt heavy. His mum was with Dominic now and his dad couldn't bear to watch anymore and had gone home all alone.

William barely had the energy to run back to take up his position for the kickoff, but fortunately for him the whistle blew for half-time a few seconds later.

The rest of the Northbrook team didn't seem too disappointed with how things were going and jogged over to the touchline and down to the changing rooms, but William had to almost drag himself off the pitch. He'd cost his team two tries and couldn't concentrate on the match at all. This was worse than he'd feared.

As he walked off the pitch, he glanced up to the crowd. Tom and Finlay were as enthusiastic as ever and waved at him. William smiled back at them. Behind Tom and Finlay, he could see someone he recognised walking along the row. The man stopped where his mum was sitting, waved at her and shook hands with Dominic, then he sat down next to them. As the man sat down, William realised it was his dad.

Mr Giles was talking to the team about tactics and how they needed to keep strong, but William wasn't listening. He couldn't stop thinking about his dad sitting down next to Dominic and his mum. Maybe he was going to have a fight with Dominic, but then why would he shake his hand? But what other reason could there be for him sitting there?

"... and go out there and do it!" Mr Giles finished his team talk and the rest of the team cheered. William realised what was happening and joined in as best he could. He stood up and started to leave the changing room with the rest of the team. Just as he was leaving, Mr Giles pulled him to one side.

"William! You ok? Not too nervous?"

"No, it's just..."

"Good. No need to be nervous. You've got the beating of their centre. You've got the skill. So don't be nervous, trust yourself and go for it!"

"Right. Ok. Thanks, Mr Giles," William said and ran out to join the rest of his teammates.

He glanced behind him, up at the stand, as he ran out and saw his mum, Dominic and his dad all chatting together. They saw him looking at them and all three of them waved. He waved back uneasily. He looked again at his dad and he was laughing at something Dominic had just said. He looked, well, relaxed was the only word William could think of. Maybe he wasn't going to punch Dominic after all. William couldn't decide if he was happy about that. Obviously, Dominic deserved a punch for, for, well, just for being Dominic, but he was glad his dad looked happy and relaxed.

William turned his attention to the match. Soon after the second half started, the Northbrook stand off had kicked the ball deep into the Mickleborough half after a scrum. William had seen what he was going to do and had got ready to chase after it. He ran as hard as he could and got to the ball first. He slid on the grass to collect the ball but was soon surrounded by players from both teams as a ruck formed.

Northbrook kept possession of the ball and played it in the forwards with a couple more rucks, before the scrum half passed it out to the left, where Northbrook had their winger and full back. However, Mickleborough only had their winger to mark them and within a couple of passes the Northbrook winger had made it to the try line. He even had chance to run close to the posts before he grounded the ball for the try, meaning the conversion was easier and Northbrook had closed the gap to 17-14.

The rest of the second half was tight. Both teams worked hard, but neither of them could make the breakthrough. The Northbrook forwards continued to play really well and they matched the bigger Mickleborough players for power. While William managed one tackle, which Alex told him had definitely saved a try.

Northbrook were trying hard to score again, but Mickleborough were keeping them out. William knew there could only be a couple of minutes left and the Northbrook players were starting to feel the tension.

William glanced up at the crowd again. Tom and Finlay were still cheering like mad. They both put their thumbs up and shouted his name. William didn't acknowledge them this time as he kept focussed on the game. But he also saw his mum wave, Dominic put his thumb up and

William's dad clapped his hands. Despite the tension of the match William felt a wave of calm pass over him.

The Northbrook forwards were playing with power and control and they had managed to move the ball forward with ruck after ruck until they were on the edge of the Mickleborough 22-metre line. They were on the right-hand side of the pitch, with the Northbrook backs - William included - lined up to the left, ready to have one last attack.

The Northbrook scrum half picked the ball out of the back of the ruck and passed it to his left. The stand off passed it left as well. The ball was now with the inside centre, on William's right. He ran a few paces forwards and then passed to his left - to William.

William knew what was expected of him, he could hear the Northbrook full back to his left calling for the ball and the winger beyond him. William should pass the ball left and hope the winger could squeeze past his marker and score a try. But William also knew Mickleborough expected it too, in fact his opposite number had already taken half a step to his right to cover the pass he thought William was going to make.

William took a step forward and moved his arms across his body from right to left, but instead of letting go and completing the pass, he brought his arms and the ball back into his chest. At the same time, he pushed off hard on his left leg and changed the direction he was running so that he was now running into the gap between the Mickleborough players on his right. The opposition centre was stranded, covering the pass that William never made, which meant William could see the try line only eight metres in front of him. He sprinted and although he could feel a tackle coming in, his momentum took him over the line and he touched the ball down. He had done it! He had scored the winning try!

The referee blew the whistle, the match was over and William had won the match for his team!

His teammates mobbed him, cheering and celebrating, but William looked up to the stand and waved. Tom and Finlay were jumping up and down with excitement and even from this far away, William could tell they were trying to tell everyone near them they were best friends with William.

Behind Tom and Finlay, Dominic was on his feet clapping, but leaning awkwardly in front of him William's mum and dad were hugging. The hug broke up and William's mum stood up straight and put her arm around Dominic, who planted a big kiss on her cheek. William's dad was jumping up and down with almost as much excitement as Tom and Finlay.

As the players came off the pitch, Harry ran up to William.

"Told you you were a good player!"

"Ha! Yeah. Thanks, Harry."

"No problem, William." Harry walked on. Then he stopped and turned back to William. "Although, you know what? You don't look like a William on the rugby pitch... so from now on, I'm gonna call you, Billy!"

THE END

259

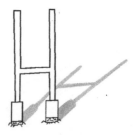

'Fiona's' Viewpoint

A view from a mother who has had similar experiences to Fiona.

I don't believe very many people start married life expecting to become a statistic. I certainly intended, once children arrived, to be in it for the long haul; but unfortunately the relationship deteriorated and I knew that if there were two unhappy adults that could only lead to two unhappy children.

It's more than 30 years since I made the hardest decision of my life. We were unusual for the time in that I became the main breadwinner, while my ex-husband became the day to day care giver. This meant I had limited contact and it was a very unusual situation for a woman to be in. I experienced social stigma and sanctions and I was very grateful to find MATCH: Mothers Apart From Their Children.

Now, I am grateful to be able to report that I have a fantastic relationship with my children. And, even after years of 'frost' from my ex, our having become grandparents recently has meant that we have more to cooperate and communicate over and hatchets appear to be well and truly buried.

I know that there will be other parents who are struggling with their own questions about whether to stay within a relationship which feels to be failing and which they know in their hearts ought to end. I say to them that as hard as it may feel, the idea of 'staying together for the children's sake' is and always has been a fallacy.

Children need happy, fulfilled parents, not martyrs. Have courage on their behalf, everyone will benefit eventually.

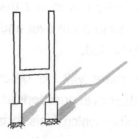

'Mark's' Viewpoint

A father who, like Mark, has been through a separation.

Separating from my wife and ultimately divorcing was a very hard time in my life. Our relationship had broken down, but I was very concerned about how it would affect my relationship with my son. If the divorce was unpleasant, would I even be able to see him?

As Mark does at the end of the book, I made it my mission to be as civil and if possible, as friendly as I could with my ex-wife. We were fortunate that we split up before things turned nasty: I wanted to make sure that they didn't descend into that. I was very lucky she wanted that too.

But deciding to behave like that and actually behaving like that are two different things and it wasn't always easy. One of the things I found most difficult was a lack of control or consultation when it came to our son. Not with the big things, we've always been able to talk about those, but the little things such as bedtimes, or whether a film is appropriate for his age.

The reverse of that though is that whenever he is with me it is my parenting style that is used. I think my ex and I have slightly different styles, but as a busy working dad (like many others) I didn't get to do much parenting as she did it all. Now, I have to do some and I love it. Hopefully he does too.

As I write this, it is several years after the split and I have a very good relationship and I would even go as far as to say friendship with my ex-wife. But most importantly of all, I have a great relationship with my son. What he doesn't realise is how much happier he is now he has two parents who are happier than they would have been if they'd stayed together.

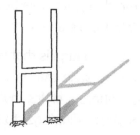

'William's' Viewpoint

The view of a boy who has experienced a parental break-up.

I don't remember my mum and dad telling me that they were splitting up - which I suppose is strange considering how important it would have been at the time. I've been told that I cried and hugged my mum when I was told the news.

One thing I do remember is when we moved house. My dad moved out first and then my mum and I moved out a few months later. I remember being sat on a chair as the removal men carried stuff out around me. I now spend time with both my mum and my dad and I like that - I like that I have two houses to live in.

Quite a lot of friends are in a similar position to me and I think it's quite normal now. No-one really talks about it as so many of us live like this. One of my best friends went through it recently, but he's ok too.

I don't like that I have to carry my stuff from house to house - like my school uniform and my school books and things - but other than that I think things are better now than they would have been. I might not have said that at the start, but it would be really weird if my mum and dad were back together again now.

If anyone else is going through this, I'd just tell them that it will all work out ok in the end. It might be upsetting at the start, but it's probably for the best and you'll get used to it all.

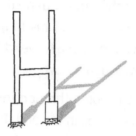

A Note from the Author

The idea for this book came to me as my ex-wife and I were separating. I've often said to people that it is the book I wanted to be able to read to my son at that time - and that is true. However, it is also the story I wanted to hear as a parent.

I wanted me and my son to know that no matter how rubbish things felt at that point in time, they would get better, we would be ok and we would actually have fun, be happy and succeed in life.

The concept for the book came as one complete scene popped into my head (I wonder if you can guess which one it is) and the rest of the book was written around that scene.

What I hope I've managed to do with this book is to show kids of divorced parents that life will be ok, but also show parents that you can help to make life ok for your kids. However, I also want to show how important friendships are and how good friends can help support people as they go through life. Everyone should strive to be a Tom or Finlay!

Points for Discussion

Changes

William goes through a lot of changes during this period of his life, how do you think he copes with it?

Does he cope well or badly? What could he do better?

Do you think he likes the changes?

Have you experienced any similar changes to William? How did you cope?

Did you have anyone who helped you?

Some ideas to get you started...

At the beginning of the book he has changed house, school and friends. Then he starts to play rugby for the first time.

Of course he has the changes to his parents' relationship to navigate, which includes a change to the Christmas routines. Not to mention his mum's new boyfriend or the changes of moving into Billy's world and back.

....

....

....

....

....

....

....

....

....

Points for Discussion

Friendship

Throughout the book William's friendship with Tom and Finlay is very important, but what makes a good friend?

Do you think William is a good friend to them?

What other examples of friendship are shown in the book?

Do people have to be the same, or like the same things, to be friends?

What makes you a good friend?

Some ideas to get you started...

William mentions friends of convenience from his old house and school. But his friendship with Tom and Finlay seems different. Would you consider Harry and Abigail William's friends?

There are other examples of friendship, including Mr Giles and the teacher at Welton school, or William's dad being friendly to Dominic.

....

....

....

....

....

....

....

Points for Discussion

Billy

We meet Billy a few times in the book, but we're never properly introduced. Who do you think Billy is?

Do you think there is a reason why Billy appears when he does?

Does Billy help or hinder William?

What is happening when William's parents are watching William (Billy) in their back garden?

If you were to meet Billy, how might he be able to help you?

Some ideas to get you started...

Billy is described as "someone much older [than William], someone maybe 19 or 20 years old."

The first time we meet him is after William's first rugby match.

Billy can already do the dummy pass that William is practising with his dad.

....

....

....

....

....

....

....

Points for Discussion

William's Parents

The relationship between William's parents is quite complicated throughout the story, how would you describe it?

Do you think that William's mum will move back in with William and his dad? What about Dominic?

How does William feel when his parents are living together? What is the relationship like when they live apart?

Maybe your parents are separated, or you have friends whose parents are separated. How does it make you feel?

Some ideas to get you started...

At the start of the book William describes hiding under the bed covers to hide from some of their arguments. They also 'whisper' a lot and have fake smiles.

William's mum was happy to invite his dad over to her flat to try and cheer William up when he was upset – they shared a bottle of wine.

How do you think they felt watching William, separately, in the back garden?

....

....

....

....

Points for Discussion

Fighting

William has a fight with Harry in the book, why do you think he does that?

Do you think that William is a natural 'fighter'?

William is in the corridor for the fight because he shouts at Tom in class, why does he shout at Tom?

How do you think the fight changes William's relationship with Harry? Why?

Why does Mr Wilson, the headmaster, treat William and Harry differently when they are sent to see him? Do you think that is fair?

What do you think Mr Wilson would say to you if you were sent to him for fighting?

Some ideas to get you started...

William talks about enjoying the tackles in rugby - even when Billy tackles the fully grown men. But, he also talks about being scared of Harry in the fight and just afterwards.

William was also very angry at that time, it may have had an impact on how and why the fight started.

....

....

....

....

....

Points for Discussion

The Zoo

William and Finlay had a great day at the zoo, which animals did they see and which did they like best?

Do you think it was important that Tom wasn't there?

Why do you think Finlay likes reading about the lizards?

Why doesn't William read more about the penguins if he loves them so much?

How does the trip to the zoo affect William's mum?

What is your favourite zoo animal?

Some ideas to get you started...

The large, adult, male monkey frightened the boys and the insects bored them. Then Finlay saw the lizards, before they watched the penguins in the water.

William and Finlay also talked about Top Trumps and rugby, while the mums chatted about other things.

....

....

....

....

....

....

....

....

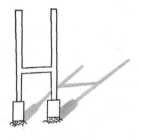

Glossary

Dummy Pass

An offensive ruse, where the ball carrier moves as if to pass the ball to a teammate, but continues to run with the ball himself; the objective is to trick defenders into marking the would-be pass receiver, creating a gap for the ball carrier to run into.

22

On the pitch there are two '22m' lines, marking 22 metres (or 72ft) from each team's try line. If a team get inside the opposition's '22' they are close to scoring a try, which creates pressure.

Advantage

The period of time after a foul or other infringement in which the non-offending side has the opportunity to benefit and the game need not be stopped due to the infringement. If no advantage is gained, the referee will blow the whistle and give the decision that had been delayed. The Advantage Law is designed to allow the game to flow more freely.

Centre

These players wear shirts number 12 (inside centre) and number 13 (outside centre). They need to be aggressive tacklers in defence and explosive runners in attack.

Conversion

When a team scores a try, they have an opportunity to 'convert' it for two further points by kicking the ball between the posts and above the crossbar - that is, through the goal. The kick is taken at any point on the field of play in line with the point where the ball was grounded for the try, parallel to the touch-lines. It is advantageous to score a try nearer to the posts as it is easier to convert it.

Flanker

Forwards whose key objective is to win possession through turn-overs, using physicality in the tackle and speed to the breakdown. They wear shirts number 6 and 7.

Fly Half

The primary role of the fly half is to organise and communicate well with the forwards and backs. The fly half, also known as the stand off, is normally the main decision maker. They choose the direction (left or right), the width (close or wide) and the depth (short or long) of the attack. The fly half wears shirt number 10.

Free Kick

A free kick is awarded for less significant offences. A team may not score points directly from a free kick. A team may opt for a scrum instead of a free kick.

Full Back

This player wears shirt number 15. The full back is expected act as the last line of defence, to field high kicks from the opposition, and reply with a superior kick or counter-attack.

Hooker

Hookers traditionally wear shirt number 2. In a scrum, they are placed centrally in the front row and use their feet to 'hook' the ball back. Hookers often throw the ball in at line outs, partly as they are the shortest of the forwards, but also because they are the most skilful of the forwards.

Interception

Gaining of possession by running forward from the defensive line and taking a pass meant for a member of the opposition.

Knock On

A knock on occurs when the ball accidentally moves forward after coming into contact with the upper body of a player, and then touches either the ground or another player. It results in a scrum to the opposition.

Late Tackle

A late tackle is a tackle executed on a player who has already passed or kicked away the ball. As it is illegal to tackle a player who does not have the ball, late tackles are penalty offences.

Line Out

When the ball has left the pitch by the sidelines it is returned to the pitch by a line out. Usually, the hooker of the team in possession throws the ball in.

Lock

The locks are forwards and are the giants of the team, combining their physicality with great catching skills and mobility. Locks win ball from lineouts and restarts. They drive forward in the scrum, rucks and mauls providing a platform for attack. Their key characteristic is height. They wear shirts number 4 and 5.

Maul

A maul occurs when the ball carrier is held by one or more opponents and one or more of the ball carrier's team mates holds on (binds) as well (a maul therefore needs a minimum of three players). The ball must be off the ground.

Number 8

Number 8 is the name of the position of the player that wears the number 8 shirt. They are a forward and their job is to secure possession at the base of the scrum, carry the ball in open play, provide the link between the forwards and backs in attacking phases and defend aggressively. Good handling skills are essential, as is a great awareness of space. Power and pace over short distances is crucial - gaining territory and field position for a quick release to the backs in attack.

Offside

If a player is further forward (nearer to the opponents' goal line) than the teammate who is carrying the ball or the team mate who last played the ball, they are offside. In itself, being offside is not an offence unless the player takes part in the play. If they do, the player will be penalised.

Passing

To transfer a ball to a teammate by throwing it. Passes in rugby must not travel forwards.

Penalty Kick

If a team commits a penalty infringement, the opposition have the option of a place kick at goal from where the infringement occurred. If successful, it is worth three points.

Prop

The props 'prop up' the hooker in the scrum. Their main role is to provide stability at the scrum and support the hooker in quickly winning the ball. They wear shirt number 1 (loosehead prop) or number 3 (tighthead prop).

Ruck

A ruck is formed when the ball is on the ground and one or more players from each team close around it. Players must not handle the ball in the ruck, and must use their feet to move the ball or drive over it so that it emerges at the team's hindmost foot, at which point it can be picked up.

Scrum

The eight forwards from each team bind together and push against each other. The scrum half from the team that has been awarded possession feeds the ball into the centre of the scrum.

Scrum Half

The scrum half is the link between the forwards and the backs. As well as feeding the ball into the scrum, their role is to keep play moving and to collect the ball from the forwards after a scrum, line out, ruck or maul and to play it out to the backs. Wears shirt number 9.

Tackle

A tackle takes place when one or more opposition players grasp onto the ball carrier and succeed in bringing him/her to ground and holding them there.

Try

This is the primary method of scoring. A try is worth five points. It is scored when a player places the ball on the ground with downward pressure in the in-goal area between (and including) the try line and the dead ball line.

Wingers

These players wear shirts number 11 and number 14 and play on the left and right edges of the pitch. Wingers must be fast runners, be agile in order to evade tackles and have excellent ball-handling skills in order to pass and receive the ball at pace.

The Rugby Pitch

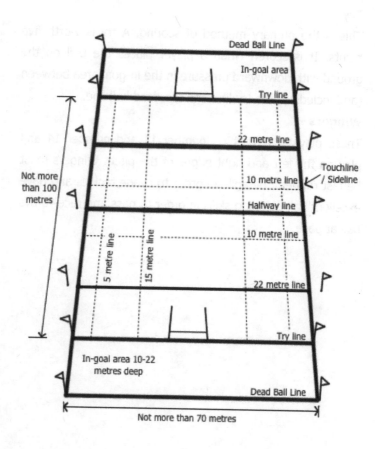

Dead Ball Line

In-goal area

Try line

22 metre line

10 metre line

Touchline / Sideline

Halfway line

10 metre line

5 metre line

15 metre line

22 metre line

Try line

In-goal area 10-22 metres deep

Dead Ball Line

Not more than 100 metres

Not more than 70 metres

Positions and Shirt Numbers

1	-	Loosehead Prop
2	-	Hooker
3	-	Tighthead Prop
4	-	Lock / Second Row
5	-	Lock / Second Row
6	-	Blindside Flanker
7	-	Openside Flanker
8	-	Number 8
9	-	Scrum Half
10	-	Fly Half
11	-	Left Winger
12	-	Inside Centre
13	-	Outside Centre
14	-	Right Winger
15	-	Full Back

Helpful Organisations

Action for Children
www.actionforchildren.org.uk

Action for Children protects and supports children and young people, providing practical and emotional care and support. They ensure their voices are heard, and campaign to bring lasting improvements to their lives.

Phone: 0300 123 2112 (open 9am to 5pm, Monday to Friday)
Email: ask.us@actionforchildren.org.uk

Childline
www.childline.org.uk

Childline helps anyone under 19 in the UK with any issue they're going through. You can talk about anything, big or small, the trained counsellors are there to support any child.

Phone: 0800 1111

Families Need Fathers
www.fnf.org.uk

Families Need Fathers seeks to obtain the best possible blend of both parents in the lives of children; enough for the children to realise both parents are fully involved in their lives. They believe that, legally, parents should be of equal status.

Phone: 0300 0300 363

Family Lives
www.familylives.org.uk

Family Lives provides targeted early intervention and crisis support to families who are struggling. The issues they support families with include: family breakdown, challenging relationships and behaviour, debt, and emotional and mental wellbeing.

Phone: 0808 800 222
Email: askus@familylives.org

Gingerbread
www.gingerbread.org.uk

Gingerbread aims for a society in which single parent families are treated equally and fairly. They provide information to help single parents support themselves and their family. They campaign and influence policy to reduce stigma against single parents, and make services more accessible to all families - whatever their shape or size.

Phone: 0808 802 0925
Email: peersupport@gingerbread.org.uk

Kids
www.kids.org.uk

Kids aims to empower disabled children and young people to develop their skills and achieve their aspirations. They create opportunities for them to take part in all aspects of life.

Phone: 0207 359 3635

Mothers Apart From Their Children (MATCH)
www.matchmothers.org

Match is a charity offering non-judgemental support and information to mothers apart from their children in a wide variety of circumstances. They believe that children have a basic human right to continue to be part of a loving, nurturing family network for life, no matter how many times a family re-makes itself, no matter where their mothers live.

Phone: 0800 689 4104
Email: enquiries@matchmothers.org

NSPCC
www.nspcc.org.uk

The NSPCC is a leading children's charity in the UK, specialising in child protection and dedicated to protecting children today to prevent abuse tomorrow. The only UK children's charity with statutory powers, which means they can take action to safeguard children at risk of abuse.

Phone: 0808 800 5000
Email: help@nspcc.org.uk

Relate
www.relate.org.uk

Relate is the UK's largest provider of relationship support, and last year they helped over two million people of all ages, backgrounds, sexual orientations and gender identities to strengthen their relationships.

Phone: 0300 0030 396

The Children's Society
www.childrenssociety.org.uk

Providing specialist support that empowers young people to make positive changes and rediscover their hope. The Children's Society works alongside young people, their families and community, and wants to create a society built for all children.

Phone: 0300 303 7000

Voices in the Middle
www.voicesinthemiddle.com

Voices in the Middle is a collaboration between young people, the family law and mediation sector and The Family Initiative charity to provide a dedicated place for young people to find help and support when in the middle of divorce and separation. Voices in the Middle is an information website and has many connections with the other organisations provided here. It is possible to use an online chat box on their website to seek help.

Young Minds
www.youngminds.org.uk

Young Minds is one of the UK's leading charities fighting for children and young people's mental health. They want to see a world where no young person feels alone with their mental health, and all young people get the mental health support they need, when they need it, no matter what.

Text: YM to 85258
Parents Helpline: 0808 802 5544

About the Author

As well as being an author, Patrick is a marketing consultant, charity director and open water swimmer. He is also a divorced father.

After graduating from Bradford University and working for and running a number of marketing agencies, Patrick rediscovered his love of writing in his late forties.

This book will be the first of many (he hopes).

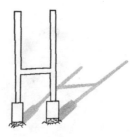

Acknowledgements

My biggest thanks go to Joshua, for being the inspiration for this book, as well as an early and enthusiastic reader. But mainly for being a great son. I'm very proud to be your dad.

A huge thanks to Liz for all your support for me and the book. You have made me believe that I am worthwhile and valid. Thank you for all you do for me.

Of course, I have to thank the early readers of the book who helped with encouragement, ideas and corrections, especially Mary, Ron, Sylvia and Tony.

Finally, a massive thank you to Abbirose of Ladey Adey Publications. Her patient cajoling, reassurance and inspiration helped to get all the words written. Then once they were, she turned them into an actual book! Thank you.